The Children of Horseshoe Hideout

in

Family Trees

Rebecca Matthews Vorkapich

To Adalynn –
I promise this one
isn't scary!
Love you!
Aunt Becky

Dedicated to Ava, Caleb, and Regan
for encouraging me to write more.

Table of Contents

Table of Contents
(continued)

~ 1 ~

THE CLEARING

The warm September sun rose slowly over the farm. Fingers of light stretched through the trees, onto the front porch, and square into Ransom's sleeping face. The blue-eyed Weimaraner stood up, stretched, then padded over to the kitchen door to wait…but not for long.

"Hey, Ransom!" Birk squatted down to give him a proper greeting. "How'd you sleep, buddy? Did you dream about rabbits? Huh? Well, let's get you some fresh water, okay?"

Ransom barked and wagged his tail, his answer to most questions.

Birk filled the water dish and watched while Ransom lapped it up. "I'm going to the clearing to feed the birds before the bus gets here. You can go with me but you have to behave. I don't want you chasing them off, okay?"

Ransom gave an eager bark.

"Right. Like I believe you." Birk chuckled. He went back in the kitchen, grabbed a breakfast bar from the snack cupboard and shoved it inside his jacket pocket. He poured a glass of milk and downed it. As he started for the pantry to fetch the bucket of bird feed, he noticed a note on the table from his dad:

We need to talk when you get home from school. Don't wander off.

"We need to talk?" Birk tried to think what they might need to talk about. "Don't we talk every night?"

Birk grabbed the bucket of feed, a treat for Ransom, and went outside. "Come on, boy. Let's go wander off."

This was Birk's favorite time of the day. The sun was cresting over the hill, rays shining through the pines and shimmering off dew drops like tiny Christmas lights. Vehicles rarely passed their house, so the only sounds–other than Ransom running after a deer or rabbit—were birdsong, chirping squirrels and a light breeze rustling through the trees. The many trees.

Birk stopped to fill the feeder by the front porch, then the one around the corner by the kitchen window. Next, on to the clearing—his favorite spot on the farm. Birk and Ransom passed row after row of carefully cultivated Christmas trees varying in size from a little over a foot tall, to way over Birk's head. And just beyond the barn was the fairy-tale forest of massive pines that sheltered Birk's clearing.

Birk would never actually call it a fairy-tale forest, of course. He'd be laughed out of sixth grade for that; but really, if Hansel and Gretel got lost here, it would be a happy place for them to wait for their dad. As soon as Birk stepped into the cool shade and onto the cushiony blanket of fallen pine needles, the fresh scents and whispering breeze seemed to transport him. Even Ransom behaved himself here...for a while.

Birk continued deeper into the woods until he could see the denser, natural forest beyond. The clearing was right where the pine woods—planted by his ancestors over a hundred years ago—met the native forest. His Grandpa Mac first showed him the clearing, and the path that led through the forest to nearby Turtle Lake.

They took many walks together through these trees, at times with the purpose of fishing in Turtle Lake, but sometimes just so Grandpa could teach Birk about the land and the trees. They often stopped to rest or to have lunch in the clearing.

Birk considered it to be his secret hideout now that his grandpa was gone. He was certain his dad had been there before, but they had never been there together. Maybe someday he would show it to his friend, Dillon. But for now, Ransom was the only friend who knew of it.

Birk set the bucket of bird feed on the ground in front of the fire pit, near the center of the clearing. He scratched the scruff of Ransom's neck. "Now, remember. You aren't supposed to scare the birds, okay?"

Ransom whined, licked Birk's hand and glanced over his shoulder at the bird feeder.

"Sit," Birk commanded. Ransom obeyed and was rewarded with a treat.

Birk filled the feeder he had hanging from a nearby pine. He'd made the feeder himself from lumber scraps found in the barn. Even though he made it for the birds, he knew the squirrels probably ate more than their share of the feed. Birk didn't mind, except they went through it pretty fast. Maybe too fast.

Birk knew that money was tight lately. He could tell when they went to the grocery store. He used to get away with adding some junk food into the cart, like frozen French fries, pizza, and doughnuts. But the last few weeks his dad would say, "better put that back" or "not this week, Birk." They used to go to town for breakfast every Saturday morning, too, but that stopped about a month ago.

Maybe tonight's talk was going to be about money. He hoped he wasn't going to get a lecture about all the bird feed they'd been going through. His Grandpa always fed the birds and he wanted to continue to care for them, just like he was caring for the trees.

Ransom suddenly stood and barked, ready to chase some unsuspecting creature.

"Come here, boy! What would you do if you caught them, anyway, huh?" Ransom had been part of the family for seven years. Birk got him the same year he started school, when they were both pups. His dad claimed he had to pay a small ransom for him. At the time, Birk didn't know the meaning of the word ransom, but it rhymed with handsome and he thought that perfectly described his dog. The name Ransom stuck.

The finches, cardinals, and chickadees were settled back at the feeder. Birk swiped at the makeshift wind chime he'd put up a few weeks ago. It was mostly from twigs and stones, but a couple pieces of silverware had made it from the kitchen onto the center of the chime. Birk liked the sound they made. He plopped down onto the moss covered log across from the fire pit. He opened his breakfast bar and ate while he watched the birds.

Birk was not a worldly traveler; other than school, an occasional football game in Iowa City, or the state fair in Des Moines, he only knew home. But he couldn't imagine too many places as peaceful as this. With the twittering birds, rustling pines, the scamper of woodland creatures, and the splash of a bass on Turtle Lake—the clearing was full of sound, yet peaceful. And it was his…well, his dad's really.

But Birk's dad never used the woods, except to cut some firewood from a fallen tree here and there. He didn't even walk through to go fishing at the lake, preferring to drive there. He referred to this part of the property as 'the bottom-forty'.

Birk recalled the first time he asked him about that reference. He thought it was confusing. "Why do you call it 'bottom-forty' when it's on a hill?" he'd asked his dad. "And it has a lot more than forty trees!"

His dad explained that it had been called that by his dad and his dad's dad. "It's called 'bottom' because it's the southern-most part of the property. And the 'forty' is because it's right around forty acres." That made sense to Birk, but he thought it deserved a better name.

Birk's thoughts were interrupted by Ransom's wet nose nudging his hand. "Just a little bit longer, okay? There's our friend the acrobat now. Be still." Birk watched overhead as a red squirrel sat perched on the limb of a white pine, tail twitching, preparing for his jump to the feeder.

"I need to get to school, so if you want me to score your jump, you better get to it," Birk whispered to the squirrel.

The squirrel appeared frozen, like a furry woodland statue, but then started to inch forward on the branch. In an instant, he was soaring through the air.

He plopped on the rim of the feeder, hanging on by his front paws. Blue, yellow, brown, and red birds flew in all directions. Seed scattered to the forest floor as the feeder swung back and forth. The squirrel scurried onto the platform to get his reward.

"Whoa! A little rough on the landing, don't you think? And look at the mess you made. Sorry, no perfect ten for you today...but a solid nine, for sure."

Birk finished his breakfast, put the wrapper in his pocket and picked up the bucket. He scratched Ransom behind the ear. "Okay, boy. Let's head back so I don't miss the bus."

Birk paused in front of the huge pine that seemed to tower over all the others--the pine that had been there for over a century. He remembered when Grandpa Mac first showed him the tree and how the names carved into the side made him feel proud of the McKenzie family trees...and still did.

~ 2 ~

AT THE NEW HIDEOUT

Hannah searched under a stack of papers at the kitchen counter as her little brother, Jamie, walked in.

"Hey, bud," she greeted him. "Mom had to go downstairs to work on a wedding cake or something. She said you can have cereal here or you can have a quiche at the bakery if you'd rather."

Jamie drummed his fingers against the counter-top and scrunched his mouth to the side. "Did she say *anything* about doughnuts?"

Hannah chuckled. "No, but if you were to eat all the quiche, I suspect she would probably let you have a doughnut *hole,* maybe. Wes is there, too. He went down early to eat with Dad."

"Okay. I'll get ready for school and then go down. What are you looking for, anyway? Is something lost that I can help you find? I still need a good mystery to solve, you know," Jamie said.

"I'm just looking for my notes on crinoids. I was going to work on my English paper during study hall today. I put them on note cards that look like…"

"Like these?" Jamie was holding up a stack of index cards.

"Jamie! What are you doing with those?"

Jamie shrugged his shoulders. "I need something like this to put notes on like real detectives do."

"Detectives use little notebooks, not index cards, and they definitely do not use their sister's schoolwork!" Hannah grabbed the cards from Jamie and plunked him on the head with them. "I probably have a notebook you can use, but ask next time, okay?"

Twelve-year-old Hannah Faris-Wheel and her younger brothers, Wes and Jamie, had been living with their adoptive parents, Robert and JoAnn Wheel for nearly a year. Prior to that, when they were the Faris children, they had run away from their cruel Aunt Olga and hid out in an old warehouse they affectionately named Horseshoe Hideout. While there, Hannah entertained Jamie by reading to him from her Nancy Drew mysteries. Not only did he become an avid reader, as a result, but he was now a big fan of mysteries. In fact, he was a little obsessed with finding his own mystery to solve.

"We have show-and-tell today and I was going to tell my class about my mystery solving business. Do you have a notebook I could take to school with me today, *please*?" Jamie asked.

Hannah picked up her backpack from the kitchen table and searched inside. She pulled out a small spiral notebook, tore out a few used pages and handed it to Jamie. "Here, nearly new. But don't let your mystery solving interfere with your schoolwork, okay?"

"Thanks, Hannah! I'm going to get dressed and go downstairs for quiche."

"Okay. I'll wait for you."

Once the children had been rescued by Robert and JoAnn, the old warehouse—Horseshoe Hideout—had been totally remodeled by Robert and his construction company, Wheel Construction. The hideout was now a series of shops and offices, but even better, their new home. The shops were on the first floor, including The Little Hideout Bakery run by JoAnn; the offices were on the second floor; and their home was on the third floor, the same floor the children had used as their hideout when they ran away.

Hannah was grateful every day to be living with Robert and JoAnn, and in such a beautiful space. She ran to her bedroom to grab a sweater and a book for English. She paused at the bedroom door and looked around at the beautiful room designed just for her. She reminded herself, again, how lucky she was to be living there...and with them. As much as she loved her biological parents and always would, she loved her adoptive parents, too.

She remembered the day a couple months ago when she and JoAnn were back-to-school shopping and she accidentally addressed her as 'Mom' instead of JoAnn. The word caught both of them by surprise. For a moment, they just stared at each other; Hannah wondering if she should correct herself, JoAnn frozen as though afraid she would.

But Hannah knew JoAnn thought of her as a daughter and she was every bit a mother to Hannah and her brothers. So, she didn't correct herself. She repeated it with finality. "Mom." They hugged in the middle of the store, Hannah accidentally whacking JoAnn on the back of her head with one of her packages, sending them both into tearful laughter.

Later that night, when Robert walked in the door from work, Hannah greeted him with a hug and one word, "Dad." He tightened his arms around her and said he liked the sounds of that. Wes jumped up and joined the hug. From that moment forward they were Mom and Dad to him, too. Jamie, on the other hand, had called them Momma Jo and Poppa Bob from the start, and didn't feel the need to change.

Hannah took one last look around her room then turned and bumped into a fully dressed Jamie. "Ready, Hannah?" he asked.

Hannah wiped the toothpaste off his cheek. "Ready. Let's go!"

There was a good crowd at The Little Hideout. Many of the office workers from the second floor stopped for coffee and pastry before work, as did the other shop owners next door. Hannah knew to get her own food when the shop was so busy.

"I'll get your breakfast, Jamie. Get a glass of milk and go sit with Wes," Hannah said. She went behind the counter to get their breakfast and peeked into the kitchen to say hello. Her mom and her mom's partner and best friend, Darlene, were making notes as they studied a picture of a wedding cake.

"Hi, Mom! Hi, Darlene!" Hannah waved. "I'm getting Jamie a quiche. Okay if I give him a doughnut hole to go with that?"

"Oh, thanks for doing that, Hannah," JoAnn said. "Make sure he finishes most the quiche first, okay? Oh, I put a smoothie in the fridge for you. Are you riding with the boys to school?"

"No," Hannah said. "Annie's mom will be picking me up. We have journalism after school so I'll be a little late, okay? She's bringing me home."

"Oh, yes. That's right. It's your first meeting on the school paper. I'll pop out to see the boys before they leave. Here's your smoothie, dear. Oh, Hannah, Curtis called and asked if Jamie might want to go with him when he takes Rusty to the dog park tonight. He'll be leaving about five. Would you mention it to him? I may get side-tracked and forget to tell him."

"Sure. He'll like that!" Hannah said.

Curtis Clipper was an elderly man that used to live next door to the Wheels before they moved to Horseshoe Hideout. He still lived very close, since Horseshoe Hideout was just across the alley from Curtis' backyard. He and Jamie became fast friends when Curtis caught the children sneaking vegetables out of the Wheel's garden when they were struggling to survive on their own.

At the time, JoAnn was running The Wheel and Deal Thrift Shop, but when she started the bakery business in the newly remodeled Horseshoe Hideout, Curtis took over running the shop. He remained close friends with the family, but especially Jamie.

Hannah glanced around the bakery and found her brothers sitting at their favorite table.

Wes had his nose buried in a book. Jamie was writing in his new 'detective' notebook.

"Here's your breakfast, bud. The quiche first, then the doughnut hole. Okay? Oh, and Curtis is taking Rusty to the dog park tonight around five and wanted to know if you'd like to go with him."

"Oh goody. Sometimes Rusty gets away from Curtis and he can't run as fast as me," Jamie said. He closed his notebook and started on his breakfast.

"You want some of my smoothie, Wes?" Hannah asked.

Wes looked up from his book. "No, thanks. I'm stuffed. I had a breakfast sandwich with Dad before he left for work."

"What are you reading there?" Hannah asked. "Do you have a test today or something?"

"No. This is just a book about chess moves." Wes closed the book and showed Hannah the cover. "We have chess club tonight so I was brushing up."

"Ah! Researching the Fools Mate to try on some poor newbie?" Hannah asked.

"No. They all know that one already. I'm trying to learn the Tennison Gambit. I'll show you when I get home."

"Oh great. Another sneak attack. Hey, did Dad

say if we're going fishing this weekend?" Hannah asked.

Fishing was a favorite pastime for the whole family, but they hadn't been able to go nearly as often as they had last fall. The Mississippi had flooded in the spring and summer, making boating impossible for months on end. Even fishing off the riverbank had been out of the question.

"I checked the river stage and it's still too high, but he said he had a surprise for us," Wes said. "I asked him if we would be going fishing somewhere this weekend. He said that might be a possibility, but he would tell us everything over dinner."

"Very mysterious!" Hannah said.

Jamie quit chewing. "It's mysterious? I need to make a note of that." He picked up his pencil and flipped the page in his notebook. "Now, tell me exactly what Dad said."

Wes gave Hannah a quizzical look.

Hannah shrugged. "He's hooked on mysteries. What can I say?"

"Dad's telling us the surprise tonight, Jamie," Wes said. "I don't think there's much to be solved."

"Hmph." Jamie went back to eating his quiche, picking up a little piece of doughnut hole with each bite.

"Jamie, wouldn't it taste better if you finished the

quiche first?" Hannah asked. "Then the doughnut hole would actually taste like a doughnut."

"No time," Wes said, as a blue van pulled up to the curb and honked. He shoved his book inside his backpack. "Our ride is here, Jamie."

Jamie dropped his fork and popped the remainder of the doughnut hole into his mouth. He smiled sheepishly at Hannah.

"Take a drink before you choke on that thing," Hannah said.

Hearing the honk, JoAnn hurried out from the kitchen, waving in their direction. "Wes, Jamie, have a wonderful day and I'll see you tonight, okay? Good luck at chess tonight, Wes! Did you find something to take for show-and-tell, Jamie?"

"I've got it covered, Momma Jo," Jamie said as he grabbed his detective notebook. "Yummy breakfast, by the way! Oh, and I'll be working on the clues of Dad's mysterious surprise."

JoAnn gave him a puzzled look, then glanced at Wes and Hannah.

"Don't ask," Wes said, rolling his eyes. "Dude, there are no clues and he's telling us tonight. Bye, Mom!"

Hannah looked at her mom and shrugged. "That's our Jamie."

~ 3 ~

DILLON'S NEWS

Birk held on to the back of the seat in front of him as the bus bounced down the gravel road. They were coming up on the Griffith farm, the closest neighbors to Birk and his dad. Birk spotted their one-eyed rooster chasing chickens all around the yard. Thankfully, he hadn't chased them into the road yet.

They pulled to a stop in front of the Anderson farm. Dillon Anderson was in fourth grade at Perkins Elementary—same school as Birk, but two years behind him. They had been sitting together on the bus for as long as Dillon had been going to school, probably because they were the last two stops before hitting the city limits. It didn't hurt that their dads were good friends, too.

Dillon climbed up the steps, greeted the driver, and slid into the empty spot by Birk.

"Hey, Birk!" he said.

"Hey, Dillon. Friday finally got here, huh? You got big plans for the weekend?" Birk braced himself for what would likely be a long-winded response. Sometimes it just took one question and Dillon's answer would take them all the way to school.

"I guess we're going up north to meet my aunt and uncle to go camping. I wish you were going with us. My cousins are all little, so I'll be like a babysitter. Oh, hey. I know. I'll wait until dark and then tell them a really scary ghost story and they'll cry like little babies and I'll get fired."

Birk laughed. "It might be worth a try."

"Anyway," Dillon continued. "Dad said we could take the kayaks out, so that'll be cool. What are you doing this weekend?"

"I hope to do some fishing at the lake, but I need to get the new seedlings ordered for spring planting. And we need to get the planting sight prepped one of these days. I need to see when Dad has time to help me with it. Cool that you're going camping, though. We haven't done that in a really long time."

"Oh," Dillon said, puzzled. "I didn't think you were going to be ordering any trees this year. That's what my dad told me. Did your dad change his mind?"

Birk studied Dillon's face. "What? He said we weren't going to order trees?"

Dillon clamped his mouth shut, biting his lips. He shrugged his shoulders, and hummed his non-verbal response for 'I don't know.'

"Yes, you do."

"I probably didn't hear him right, Birk. You know

how I talk when I should be listening. Anyway, your dad would tell you himself if that was the case, right?"

So that's the talk we're going to have tonight.

Dillon inhaled and opened his mouth to say more, but Birk turned his head to stare out the window. They were quiet the rest of the ride.

When the bus pulled up in front of their school, Dillon eagerly grabbed his backpack to make his exit. "See you after school, Birk. Oh, wait. I have chess club so I'll be on the late bus. See ya Monday."

"Yeah. Have fun camping."

Birk didn't feel much like school, suddenly. He knew business was slow at Flinthills Cabinets, where his dad worked, but even though others had lost their job, his dad was still working. Why skip the tree order this year? It was important to the Christmas tree business that they keep planting new trees every year. They always prepared the soil and ordered the stock in the fall for spring planting. If they didn't get their order in soon, next year could be too late. He couldn't remember his grandpa ever missing a fall order.

"Mr. McKenzie, what's with the worried look?"

Birk looked up. "Oh, morning, Miss Barrett." He realized he'd been walking in a trance all the way to his first class—English with Miss Barrett.

"Mr. Nadler," Miss Barrett said. "Once again, would you kindly remove that cap?"

Birk looked behind him to see Nick Nadler, the class clown, remove his signature purple baseball cap. He needed to be reminded nearly every day to take it off. Just another way to get the attention he seemed to crave.

Birk glanced back at the sea of faces in front of him. Most everyone was chatting with someone or getting paper out of their backpacks. They all looked happy and care-free. Hannah was chatting with Annie, but looked up at him and smiled. He gave her a quick smile and took his seat across the aisle from her. He would try to focus on school until he got home.

"Happy Friday, class!" Miss Barrett said. "Today

we'll be hearing from each of you on the subject of your research paper. Remember, it needs to be related to nature. We'll go around the room, starting here with Daniel. Please stand and tell us the subject of your paper, Daniel, and why you chose it."

Daniel had chosen the Mississippi River for his subject. Miss Barrett figured this would be the most popular topic for the room, since it was the most popular natural resource in the area. "That's a big subject, Daniel. What specifically about the river?"

"Oh, I'm going to talk about the history of flooding, Miss Barrett," he said.

"Fine," Miss Barrett said, then continued to listen while the next fifteen students also choose a topic relating to the river. "Let's hear from Birk now," she said.

Birk stood. "I'm going to report on the history of our tree farm, Miss Barrett. I chose it because I knew everybody else would do the river." The class erupted in laughter. "I also chose it because it was started by my great-great-grandfather over a hundred years ago when he first came here from Scotland. He planted a pine forest on the land and that inspired my grandfather to create the Christmas tree farm."

"Thank you, Birk. We look forward to learning more about it. I'm sure a lot of those details are in your head, but I do want you to do some more traditional research, too. Students, remember that all of your papers are to include a bibliography with a listing of the source references you used. I want to see the start of your bibliographies by end of the class Monday. Okay, Ava, you're next, dear."

Birk zoned out. He wondered if his countless seedling catalogs would work as a reference. Probably not, but he had three generations of family journals at his disposal. Those would be a good source. He could also provide some details about the species of each tree he'd been planting since he was very young. He'd dig around on the internet tonight to get a list of possibilities. *Tonight.* Birk wasn't looking forward to tonight and the talk he would be having with his dad. But his attention suddenly returned to sixth grade English when Miss Barrett called on the next student.

"Hannah, what subject did you choose?" Miss Barrett asked.

Hannah stood up between her desk and Birk's. She smiled briefly at Birk then turned to the front of the room. "I'm going to report on crinoids, Miss Barrett." That caused a stir in the class and a comment from Nick Nadler.

"Crinoids?" Nick said. "I think my brother had his removed with his tonsils." After the giggling stopped, he continued. "Isn't that the wrong kinda nature, Miss Barrett?" More laughter.

"Nick, I'm guessing your brother had his *adenoids*

removed. Why don't we let Hannah explain."

Birk noticed Hannah's face turning a rosy red. *Sometimes Nick didn't know when to shut up.*

"Crinoids are marine animals, related to starfish," Hannah said. "Their fossilized remains are in the limestone deposits we see all around Flinthills. There are a lot of them in Burlington, too, which is called the Crinoid Capital of the World."

"I hate to be the one to tell you this, Hannah, but starfish live in oceans, not rivers," Nick argued.

Reluctantly, Birk thought Nick made a valid point.

"Right," Hannah started. "This area of the world used to be at the bottom of a shallow sea."

"What? Cool!" Nick said.

"Yes, very cool, Hannah," Miss Barrett interrupted. "We look forward to hearing more about crinoids."

Hannah plopped into her chair and glanced at Birk. Her exhale was audible. He knew how much Hannah disliked talking in front of the class. She always did a good job, but not without suffering through a red face that almost completely camouflaged her freckles. She sometimes forgot to blink, too, so her huge green eyes would be frozen like a deer staring into headlights. He smiled and gave her a thumbs up to let her know she did a good job. *There. She finally blinked.*

Birk was aware of the stories about Hannah and her brothers running away from their mean aunt. The aunt was charged with several crimes relating to her treatment—or rather, mistreatment—of the children. Her trial was to start soon--nearly a year after her arrest. According to the stories, Hannah had a big role in getting them away from the monster aunt. They hid out for weeks before they were found—or before Hannah found help—whichever it was. Those details were sketchy, but he knew Hannah had done a lot braver things than talk in front of a class.

~ 4 ~

SCHOOL NEWS

Hannah wished that for once she could stand up and talk in front of a group without her face turning red. Ugh! How embarrassing. She might as well be wearing a neon sign that flashed 'I'm afraid to talk! I'm afraid to talk!' At least the class seemed interested in her choice of subject, though she would prefer it if Nick were a little less interested.

Crinoids were pretty cool. Hannah was pleased that her classmates didn't seem familiar with them. It would be fun sharing all she had learned about crinoids and how they came to be. She would even include some drawings so they would know what to look for next time they encountered a chunk of limestone along the Mississippi.

Her classmate, Birk, was going to report on his family's Christmas tree farm. She hoped he would let her read it when he was done. She knew he rode the bus to school, so of course he lived out in the country, but she had no idea he lived on a Christmas tree farm. It sounded magical to Hannah.

The rest of the school day raced by. Hannah went to her locker to pick out the books she would need for homework over the weekend. She shoved them into her backpack then went to the journalism room for their first meeting on the school paper.

Annie was already there. "Hey, girl. Sit by me!" she said. Besides Hannah and her best friend, Annie, there were five other sixth graders who volunteered to work on the paper. Hannah had at least one class with each of them, so knew them all by name.

Their journalism teacher, Mr. Galvin, was in charge of the group. "Okay, everyone. Let's get started. The Perkins Chronicle is usually printed on the second Friday of the month. To offset our expenses, we sell advertising, so we'll need two of you to meet with area businesses to sell advertising every month. We'll also need one or two photographers, and the rest will be doing stories—whether covering sporting events, art shows, student council meetings, musicals, or general human interest.

"Does anyone feel strongly about where they would like to focus their energy? Yes, Bryan?"

"I'd like to be one of the photographers and I can cover some of the sporting events," Bryan said.

"Great," Mr. Galvin said, as he made a notation in a notebook. "Who else?"

Lucas raised his hand. "I'll shoot pictures with Bryan."

"Okay, that takes care of the photography," Mr. Galvin said.

Hannah raised her hand.

"Yes, Hannah."

"I could work on the advertising." Hannah knew a lot of business owners that worked in Horseshoe Hideout, as she still called it. She also hoped to be able to use her artwork in some of the ads.

"Great. Anybody want to team up with Hannah on ads?"

Annie's hand darted into the air. "Me! I will, Mr. Galvin."

"Great. Hannah and Annie on advertising then. Here's a list of costs related to the space of the ad and a sample page from one of last year's papers to give you an idea of the format we've used in the past."

Mr. Galvin continued to instruct them all on deadlines and assignments. He gave everyone a handout to further explain the process and to share contact information. The meeting went on for another thirty minutes while he gave everyone their first assignment and described the editing process each piece would undergo.

"This is going to be so fun, Hannah!" Annie said. With the meeting over, they walked down the main corridor of the school toward the exit where Annie's mother would be waiting. "Should we start calling on places this weekend?"

"Sure. I want to chat with Mom about contacting the businesses next to the bakery. Maybe Dad has some ideas, too. Do you want to come over tomorrow and—".

"Excuse me, Hannah?" Mrs. Penrose, Jamie's first grade teacher, had just stepped into the hallway in front of Hannah and Annie.

"Yes, Mrs. Penrose?"

"I'm sorry to interrupt you girls, but I heard you in the hall and was wondering if I could give you my phone number and ask that you have your mom or dad give me a call tonight?"

"About Jamie?" Alarm bells were going off in Hannah's head. "Did he do something wrong?"

"Everything is fine! Really. I just need to have a chat with your parents. It won't take long. Thanks, Hannah."

~ 5 ~

MORE BAD NEWS

Birk was not surprised when Ransom ran out to the bus to greet him after school. That was his normal behavior, and Birk loved it. He was surprised, however, that his dad's truck was in the drive. He usually got home at least an hour after Birk, although it occurred to Birk that the times had been a little irregular lately.

Mick, Birk's dad, was seated at the kitchen table when he entered the house.

"Hi, Dad. You're home early."

"Sit down, son." Mick pointed to the chair across from him at the kitchen table. "I poured you a lemonade."

Birk plopped his backpack by his chair and sat down. "We're just going to jump right into it, huh?"

Mick gave Birk a strange look. "Yeah. I just need to get this over with. I've been keeping things from you, hoping they would get better, but now I just need to say what has to be said."

Birk set the glass of lemonade back on the table without taking a sip. It was then he realized how tired his dad looked. "Are you sick, Dad?"

"No! I'm fine, Birk. I feel fine…it's just work." Mick hesitated, but continued. "I was let go at the cabinet shop a couple weeks ago. Orders were down to the point where they were just keeping a skeleton crew, but now they are shutting down completely."

That didn't make sense. "A couple weeks ago? But you've been going to work every day," Birk said.

"No," Mick said. "I've been *looking for work* every day. I was hoping I could find something right away and then I wouldn't need to have this conversation with you. Well, I have found work, but unfortunately, it is in Dubuque which means a lot of driving. It also means a cut in my pay. We have to watch our spending anyway we can, in fact..."

Birk interrupted. "Why don't you just make your cabinets here, Dad? You could use the barn for your workshop. And we could work on the trees together and maybe get even more trees."

Mick gave him a sad looking smile. "I wouldn't be able to make enough for us to live off of, Birk. It's just a hobby—my woodworking and the trees. We make enough money every year to allow us to plant new trees and maintain our stock and tools and put some money away for your college fund. It's not enough to pay the bills."

"But this place has been in our family a long time. Isn't everything already paid for?" Birk asked.

"The land is paid for, but this house was put up by your grandpa and me. I still owe on it. And we still have to pay property taxes on all the land, even if it is paid for. Not to mention the fact that we like to eat and wear clothes." Mick smiled, but his eyes didn't even crinkle.

"How far will you have to drive?" Birk asked.

"Dubuque is about a two and a half hour drive from here, so five hours round trip. It will seriously cut into our time together. I'm sorry about that, but I'll keep looking for something closer. And speaking of all that driving, I need to get the truck into the shop tomorrow before I start on Monday. There's some maintenance I've been neglecting. With the extra driving I'll be doing, I really can't put it off any longer."

"Is it another cabinet shop or a furniture maker?" Birk knew woodworking was his dad's favorite thing to do. Their house was full of beautiful pieces of furniture that he had made. Maybe he wouldn't mind the extra drive so much if he could work with wood all day.

"I'm afraid not. It's a factory job. I needed to take what they were offering."

"You don't even get to build things, anymore? You're going to hate it, Dad."

"I'll be fine. Anyway, that's not for you to worry about. But Birk, with the cut in pay, I can't justify us spending any money on a new tree order this year."

"Yeah, I heard," Birk said.

"What do you mean, 'you heard'?"

"Dillon told me on the bus this morning."

"That kid. Now why would Boone even say anything to him? He knows what a yapper his kid is. I only told Boone what was going on so he could check in on you. You're going to be alone out here for hours on end and they live close by. If you need anything when I'm not here, you call Boone, okay?"

"I'll be fine. I've got Ransom to keep me company, so you don't need to worry about me."

Birk felt bad that his dad had to do so much driving, *and for a job he'll probably hate.* But he also felt bad knowing that he couldn't place his seedling order when they usually did and that his dad wouldn't be around to help him with the trees. He kept that to himself, though. He didn't want his dad to feel worse than he already did. Besides, maybe they could still order the trees in the winter. They wouldn't have first pick at the best seedlings, *but it's not the end of the world.*

"There's one more thing, Birk," his dad said, looking down at his lemonade glass, wiping off the condensation.

"What?" Birk asked. *This is when he tells me to stop feeding the birds.*

Mick rubbed his forehead and took a deep breath. His hesitation was starting to alarm Birk.

"Just say it," Birk said.

"The money situation isn't good, Birk. I had to sell off the bottom-forty."

~ 6 ~

SURPRISING NEWS

Hannah cornered Jamie as soon as she got home from her school paper meeting. "Jamie! What did you do that would make Mrs. Penrose need to talk to Mom and Dad?"

"What? I don't know," Jamie shrugged. "Why? What did she say?"

"She said she needs to talk to Mom and Dad about you."

"I don't know, Hannah," Jamie said. "I'm a model student. Maybe she wants to tell them that."

JoAnn popped her head out of the laundry room. "What's all the commotion out here?"

Hannah handed her the note. "Mrs. Penrose wants you to call her. Obviously, about Jamie."

"I wish she would have called me and kept you out of it, Hannah. I know you've been the sister longer than I've been the mom, but this is for me to handle. So, quit frowning. Have a snack with your brother and a nice *brother-sister* chat. Okay?"

"Okay. Sorry, Jamie. I didn't mean to jump on

you. Milk?"

"Please," Jamie said.

Hannah glanced over her shoulder to be sure they were alone. "But just one thing. Did you disrupt the class with your mystery business?"

"No, Hannah. All I did was tell everyone at show-and-tell that I could help them with any mysteries they might have. Jeepers! We're allowed to talk at show-and-tell, you know?"

Hannah turned her head away from Jamie, trying to hide her smile. "Well, did anyone have any mysteries?"

"Nothing good." Jamie got out his detective notebook and flipped through it. "Percival wants to know why Mrs. Penrose makes us sing a get well song whenever one of our classmates is out sick. I'll never be able to answer that one. They're at home in bed and can't hear us singing, so what's the point?" Jamie rolled his eyes.

Hannah chuckled. "Who knows!"

"Marcy wanted to know if lightening bugs light up during the day. Willie wanted me to find out why his older sister puts lotion on her upper lip. Right here in the mustache area."

Hannah snorted. "Yeah, they aren't great mysteries, are they? You could research the lightening bugs on the internet, but so could Marcy."

Jamie slammed his notebook shut. "This is not what I was hoping for."

Wes and Robert arrived home just as JoAnn returned from her phone call. Everyone started talking at once.

"Hi, Poppa Bob!" Jamie called.

"Hi, kids. How's everyone tonight?" Robert said.

"Oh, how was chess club, Wes?" JoAnn asked.

"What did Mrs. Penrose say about Jamie, Mom?" Hannah asked.

"Mrs. Penrose called?" Robert asked.

JoAnn put up her hands for silence. "Hold it. Why don't you all wash up for dinner and we'll catch up with everyone's news when we sit down."

With order restored and dinner served, Hannah shared her news about the school paper and asked her mom and dad for help finding advertising customers.

"I don't think your classmates would be very interested in the construction company, but we'll buy an ad for the bakery," Robert said. "You should talk to the folks at the bookstore and art supply store, too."

"Good idea. Thanks, Dad," Hannah said.

"How'd you do at chess tonight, Wes?" JoAnn asked.

"Yeah, did you trick anybody with the Tennison Gambit?" Hannah asked.

"No. My opponent didn't move the way I wanted him to, so it didn't work. It was a good game though." Wes chuckled. "As long as I don't get beat in the first five moves, it's a good game."

"Anytime you want to play a practice game, Wes, let me know," Robert said.

"Thanks, Dad. Hey, what was the surprise you had for us?" Wes asked.

"Oh, right. We'll get to that, but what is this business about Mrs. Penrose and Jamie?" Robert asked.

Jamie suddenly quit chewing.

"Or, should we discuss it after dinner so nobody gets an upset stomach?" Robert said, looking from JoAnn to Jamie.

"No. It was nothing upsetting at all," JoAnn said. "She is concerned that Jamie may be a little bit bored because he is reading beyond the level she's teaching. She suggested that he spend an hour a day in an advanced reading class they have in the library. She feels Jamie would benefit from it."

"See, Hannah! She didn't say anything about my mystery business," Jamie said.

JoAnn cleared her throat. "Well, actually, she did. She said you have been a little disruptive in class, but she feels it is because you finish your reading and workbook assignment so fast. From now on, it would be best if you save your mystery discussions for recess or after school, okay?"

Jamie dropped his head and stirred his vegetables. "Okay. Sorry. I don't have any good mysteries to work on, anyway."

Hannah patted him on the back, sorry that she had snapped at him earlier.

"Well, I heard about a mystery today," Robert said.

"What?" Jamie started to push away from the table. "Let me get my notebook."

"Sit still, Jamie. You aren't going to work on this mystery," Robert said. "I don't know if you remembered this, but your Aunt Olga's trial was supposed to start in a couple weeks. She's been living at her house while she's out on bail, but now she's disappeared."

"Disappeared?" Wes and Hannah said in unison.

"What's 'out on bail'?" Jamie asked. "I thought that's when you use a bucket to get water out of your boat."

"A different kind of 'bail', Jamie. It means she was allowed to live at home while she waited for her trial date. They trusted her not to leave."

"If her trial isn't for a couple of weeks, then how can they say she's missing?" Hannah asked.

"She missed an important meeting with her lawyer. When he couldn't reach her, he went to her home--more than once--and finally alerted the authorities. She's gone."

"Did they check bingo?" Jamie asked. "She goes there a lot. And Joe's Hamburg Inn. She went there plenty."

Robert chuckled. "Yes, they've checked everywhere, Jamie. They're sure she's left town and probably the state. She left a strange note behind. She said she was leaving the house to you three. She signed it and dated it a month ago."

Hannah, Wes, and Jamie all exchanged puzzled looks.

"Why would she do that?" Hannah asked.

"We don't want that house," Wes said. "We hated that house and she hated us, so why would she do that?"

"Is it really her signature?" JoAnn asked.

"They compared the handwriting to her signature that her lawyer has on file. It's hers," Robert said. "They think she probably did it so nobody would look for her and maybe forgive her for her mistreatment of you three."

"Oh, man! I could have checked the handwriting for you," Jamie said.

Wes looked at Jamie. "Maybe you want to try to figure out where she went," he said.

"No way!" Jamie said. "If I figured out where she went then they would bring her back. Good riddance! I hope she never comes back. Don't *anybody* tell the police that she drives a big blue Buick, 'cause then they'll find her for sure."

Robert looked at JoAnn, trying to hide his grin.

"Well, there you have it," JoAnn said. "I agree with Jamie, but wherever she is, she should never be in charge of children again."

"I knew you wouldn't want the house, but we could put it up for sale and whatever money you make could go to charity." Robert said.

"That sounds nice," Hannah said.

"Or we could turn it over to the city. Maybe they could use it as a homeless shelter," Robert said.

"I like that idea even better," Hannah said.

"I agree!" Wes said. "That's what we should do. Because we were homeless once and it was her fault, so that would be good pay-backs."

Robert smiled. "If everyone agrees, then I'll check

to see what's involved in turning it over to the city."

"Agree!" they all said in unison.

"Was that the surprise you were going to tell us about?" Wes asked.

"Oh, no! I almost forgot," Robert said. "You know how we haven't been able to do any fishing because of the floods this year?"

Wes looked hopeful. "Yes?"

"Well, your mom and I thought it would be nice to buy a little patch of land near a lake, so we could still fish and boat and even swim, if we want."

"Wow! Wes said, exchanging smiles with Hannah and Jamie. "That's awesome!"

"Sweet!" Jamie said.

"Did you buy it already? Can we see it?" Hannah asked.

"We're going to pack a picnic and go see it tomorrow," JoAnn said, smiling.

"Is it far?" Wes asked.

"Not far at all," Robert said. "It's just outside the city limits, maybe a fifteen to twenty minute drive from here. Have you ever been to Turtle Lake?"

~ 7 ~

LOSING IT

Birk was stunned. Surely, his dad didn't mean what he just said. "You sold the bottom-forty?" Birk felt like throwing up.

"I had no choice, Birk. But we still have the tree farm and the barn."

"So what? You sold the whole pine forest that our family planted. And you sold the old forest and the lake access? You sold my—." Birk stopped himself. He decided his secret hideout would stay a secret.

"Your what?"

"Nothing. The forest was my favorite, Dad. You knew that. And that was our private access to the lake."

"We don't need a private access to the lake. We can drive to the public access. It's just a short drive from here."

"Yeah. Like that's the same." Birk pushed back from the table, scraping the chair across the floor. Ransom appeared outside the screen door, barking as though ready to defend Birk. But Ransom wouldn't be able to help this time. Birk stormed out of the house, screen door slamming behind him.

"Birk!" Mick shouted from the porch. "We need to talk about this!"

Birk kept walking—stomping, really—then took off running. He and Ransom ran through the farm, past the Christmas trees and into the tall evergreens that had been in the family for over a hundred years.

Tears burned Birk's eyes, branches scraped his arms. He felt so much hurt and anger, it was hard to breathe. Finally, he entered the clearing. Birds scattered in all directions. The acrobatic squirrel ran up a pine until he was out of sight. Birk kicked at the stones circling the fire pit he had built with care. He yanked on the home-made wind chime, pulling it to the ground.

Ransom made a whining sound as he watched Birk try to destroy what he took such care to create. There was no sense of quiet and calm in the clearing tonight.

"How could he do that?" Birk yelled. "How could he sell our land? Now some stranger's gonna come in and cut down all these trees. They'll ruin everything!"

Ransom barked in agreement.

"He doesn't care! He wouldn't do this if Grandpa was still alive!"

Birk kicked the stack of firewood he had piled by the fire pit. The motion caused him to lose his balance and fall forward on the stone pit. One of the stones had a sharp edge that cut through his jeans and into the flesh of his shin. The pain was immediate and intense.

"Ow!" Birk winced. He sat back and grabbed his shin with both hands. He glanced at the stone where he'd fallen. *No wonder it hurt so bad.* He didn't want to look at the damage. He would just hold it until it stopped hurting. Then he would look.

Ransom slowly approached Birk and brushed his nose against Birk's arm. Birk let go of his leg and wrapped his arms around Ransom, burying his face into the scruff of his neck. Soon, he felt a warm trickle run down his shin and into his shoe. He pressed both hands onto the wound and felt the warm stickiness ooze through his fingers.

Birk looked around for something to wrap around his leg. He needed to get home, but he wouldn't be able to hold his hands over the wound while he walked. He looked at Ransom's collar, but decided it would be too small. His own belt might work if he could tie it, but he wasn't sure he could handle that one-handed. He had to keep pressure on the wound.

He slowly removed his right hand, untied his shoe, slipped it off, then pulled off his sock. He doubled the sock over and pressed it into the wound. He pulled at the shoestring until it was free from the shoe. He used the shoestring to tie the sock securely to his leg. He slipped the shoe on and slowly stood up.

Birk wiped the tears off his face and took one last look over his shoulder. The clearing was silent. No peaceful birdsong or rustling pines to calm him. It was silent and it was a mess.

"Say goodbye, Ransom. This isn't ours anymore."

* * *

Birk limped home to find his dad at the stove cooking hamburgers. He tried to sneak past him to the bathroom.

"Get the chips out and pour some milk, please," his dad said.

Birk stopped. "You know they'll probably cut down those old trees, don't you? They've been there for centuries. We could have protected them. Then they'll cut down the pines that our family planted and you're just going to let them."

Mick flipped the burgers. "Now, Birk, you don't know that. This guy is not some lumberjack. He just wants a place to take his family to fish and swim. The lake access is perfect for that."

Birk snorted. "Yeah. I know. It was perfect. Who did you sell it to?"

"It's nobody I know so you wouldn't know him. I worked with a realtor on the sale. The buyer has a construction company of some kind."

"Construction company? That's just great! So he's going to cut down the trees and use them to build his houses!" Birk was starting to panic. "What's his name? You signed papers, didn't you? So you know his name."

Mick slid the skillet off the stove and turned around. "There's no reason you need to know that and I'm a little bit bothered by the fact you think you do."

"So I'll know who to hate instead of you!" Birk blurted out the words without thinking, sorry he had as soon as they were said. He tried to shuffle out of the kitchen—partly in shame and partly because he could feel his leg was still bleeding.

But he was too late. Mick finally noticed the bloody sock tied onto Birk's shin, the blood stain on his shoe, and his bloody hands. "Birk! Is that *your* blood?"

"Yeah. I tripped."

"Sit down. Let me see." Mick pulled out a chair for Birk to sit in.

Birk headed towards the stairs. "I'm going to go shower."

"That's a lot of blood, Birk. Sit down. It may need stitches."

Birk ignored him and hobbled up the stairs.

* * *

His leg reminded him of what a cutting board

looked like after cleaning a fish. *Gross!* Dried blood and fresh blood covered his shin. He could see that there was a gash about two inches across. A loose flap of skin barely covered the wound. It would need cleaning before he could tell how bad it really was, but it was bad enough to make him feel a little nauseous. He climbed into the shower and washed the wound as best he could. No way was he going to scrub it—he wouldn't even touch it with soap. He hoped the hot water was enough to get it clean.

He shut off the water and toweled off. He pressed the towel into his leg until the bleeding slowed to a trickle. He found a box of bandages in the medicine cabinet, and applied them one by one until the wound was covered. He stuck another row on top of the first one to be sure.

He threw on some shorts and a t-shirt and stood at the top of the stairs, listening for his dad. He was hungry but he didn't want to sit across from him at the table and pretend to enjoy his company. He just wanted to be alone. His growling stomach wouldn't let him wait any longer, so he went downstairs. His burger was still in the pan with the lid on it, so still warm. He could hear the rhythmic creaking of the porch swing so knew his dad was outside. *Good. He could eat alone.* Ransom appeared at the screen door, wagging his tail, but Birk ignored him for now.

He ate some of his dinner, but discovered he

wasn't really that interested in food. He set aside the rest of his burger for Ransom, then scraped the chips into the trash. As he started to rinse his plate, his dad came back inside.

"Sit down and let me see your leg, Birk."

"It's fine. I have it bandaged."

"Did you put any antibiotic ointment on it first?"

"No, but I cleaned it in the shower. It's fine."

"I'm taking the truck into town first thing to get it serviced. We can stop at urgent care to have them look at your leg, then get some breakfast at Dewey's while we wait for the truck."

Birk felt a tiny pang of guilt as he answered. "I need to stake up some saplings, so I'll pass." He didn't like hurting his dad's feelings, but he was hurt, too, and not very good at pretending otherwise. He filled the sink with sudsy water and started washing dishes, never giving his dad a glance.

Birk heard his dad leave the room and go into the hall bathroom. He came back to the kitchen and slapped something onto the table. "I'll do the dishes tonight. Sit down and put this ointment on your leg. You shouldn't be standing up."

* * *

Birk had a fitful night trying to sleep. He was both angry and sad about losing the bottom-forty. He was also troubled about hurting his dad's feelings, knowing that they wouldn't have much time to be together starting Monday. *Well, he hurt my feelings by selling the land.*

Birk was still a little troubled about no tree order for the fall. In the past they always ordered in the fall to ensure the best seedlings would be shipped for spring planting. If they had to wait to order in January, the best stock would likely be gone, and they would have to pay more for what they got. *But what if Dad decided they couldn't order in January, either? Was he going to slowly let the tree farm business die out?*

Birk tried to make his mind go blank so he could sleep, but then his leg would start to throb and the cycle of troubled thoughts started all over. Eventually, he did sleep because he woke to the sound of his dad's truck rumbling down the gravel drive.

~ 8 ~

THE WAY TO TURTLE LAKE

Hannah called Annie Saturday morning to let her know that they would need to meet on the school paper assignment later in the afternoon.

"We're going to check out some property near Turtle Lake. I'll call you when we get home, okay?" Hannah said.

"Lucky you! Mom needs me to teach her how to use her new laptop. This is going to be torture. I'll talk to you when you get home, Hannah."

There was an air of excitement in the Wheel household as they all prepared for the family trip to the lake. After breakfast, Robert and Wes went down to the garage to load up the fishing gear. Hannah put on a pair of denim cut-off shorts, her peace-sign t-shirt and favorite green sneakers. She pulled her hair back into a ponytail while she walked down the hall to check on Jamie. She was greeted with his pajama clad bottom sticking up in the air, his head buried under his bed.

She snickered. "Are you hiding or looking for something?" she asked.

Jamie pulled his head out from under the bed. "I can't find my lucky fishing hat!"

"Hmmm. Sounds like you have a mystery on your hands."

Jamie's serious expression suddenly turned into a smile. "You're right! I can figure this out." Jamie tapped his finger against his lip. "The last time I wore it was the last time we went fishing which was a long time ago."

"Right, so far," Hannah said.

"And Momma Jo made me clean my room since then and she says 'a place for everything and everything in its place'."

"That she does," Hannah said.

"Wait, Hannah! Don't say it." Jamie ran into his closet and pulled his hat down from the peg where he always put it when ordered to clean his room. "Ta da!"

Hannah laughed. "Good job, master sleuth! But the real mystery is why you were looking for a hat when you haven't even changed out of your pajamas!"

"I'll be ready in thirty seconds," he said.

Hannah walked into the kitchen where JoAnn was filling a picnic basket and cooler. "Hey, Mom. Should we bring swimsuits, or should we just plan on fishing this time?"

"Let's grab swimsuits and towels just in case. It's such a beautiful day. If the fish aren't biting we can put away the poles and go for a swim."

Jaime strolled in ready for the day.

JoAnn looked over the contents of the picnic basket and cooler. "Okay, I've got sandwiches, drinks, chips, berries and there was something else I wanted to take. Now what was it?"

"Dessert?" Jamie asked.

Hannah and JoAnn laughed. "I can always count on you to remember the sweets, can't I?" JoAnn said.

"You can count on me, Momma Jo!"

"Let's get our suits and towels and get this show on the road, shall we?" JoAnn said.

* * *

As soon as they exited the city limits, the rolling farmland came into view. The patches of corn and bean fields were separated by clumps of trees giving a quilt-like affect to the scene.

This would make a great painting, Hannah thought.

About fifteen miles down the highway, Robert made a left turn onto a narrow, gravel road.

"Uh oh! Watch out for the chickens!" Jamie called

from the back seat.

"Look. There's a rooster chasing them," Wes said.

A tidy farmhouse and barn stood on the left side of the road. Hannah noticed the 'Anderson' mailbox at the side of the road.

"That might be where Dillon lives," Wes said. "I know he rides the bus, because he takes the late bus after chess club."

"Have you played him yet?" Hannah asked, but she was temporarily distracted by the farm a ways down the road on the right. The farmland suddenly turned into rolling hills of evergreen trees planted in neat rows.

Jamie noticed them, too. "Look at the Christmas trees!" he said.

"They're so pretty! Oh! It's a Christmas tree farm!" Hannah turned her head quickly to try to read the name on the mailbox.

"What did that mailbox say?" she asked.

"It said McKenzie," Wes said.

"That has to be where Birk McKenzie lives," Hannah said. "He's doing his English paper on his family's Christmas tree farm."

Robert glanced at Hannah in the rear-view mirror. "You know a McKenzie, Hannah?" he asked.

"I know Birk. He's in my English and science

class."

"I purchased this property from a McKenzie. It must be his dad."

The news instantly troubled Hannah. She watched the trees outside the window flash by. They reminded her of a picture she once saw in an old book of fairy tales.

"It's like a Hansel and Gretel forest," she said.

"Yep. There's a beautiful pine forest on part of the land," Robert said.

Oh no. Didn't Birk say something about the woods being in his family for over a hundred years?

They started to slow down now. Part of the road swung off to the left, but they continued to go straight. Soon, they came to a break in the trees. Robert made a slow, sharp turn to the right and finally came to a stop.

"We're here!" Robert said.

Three heads in the back seat all converged in the middle to look at the view through the windshield. The sun-speckled lot had trees on both sides, but straight ahead was a sandy bank leading into a broad expanse of water. The lake was so calm, it was like a mirror reflecting the blue sky, white clouds and mass of trees on the opposite shore. A dock jutted out from the property into the lake.

"Oh, wow! This is so cool!" Wes declared. "You just know that lake is full of hungry fish!"

"It's beautiful," Hannah agreed. "And so private."

"Let's go have a closer look," Robert said. He shut off the car and they all piled out.

Jamie and Wes ran for the lake. Hannah walked slowly, turning in a circle to take it all in.

"Why would anyone want to sell this?" Hannah asked nobody in particular, and then looked at her dad. "Which direction is the pine forest that you bought? Is it that way or that way?" Hannah needed to know that they hadn't bought Birk's family trees.

Robert hesitated. "You're free to go into the woods either way, Hannah, just don't go in too far. You could get lost. The pine forest and most of the forty acres that we bought is in that direction." He pointed to the right—the direction they had just come from. "But don't you want to fish?"

"Oh no," Hannah gulped.

"Is something wrong?" Robert asked.

"Yes," Hannah said.

"Yes, something's wrong?" Robert repeated.

"Yes, I want to fish. I don't want the woods. I mean, I don't want to go into the woods."

And I don't want the woods.

~ 9 ~

A PAINFUL SATURDAY

Birk decided he might as well get up, since sleep wasn't likely to return. He sat up to swing his legs to the side of the bed, but stopped when he felt a stabbing pain. He'd forgotten about his leg. *How could it hurt worse today than yesterday?* Using his hands to slowly lift the wounded leg over the side of the bed, Birk was shocked to see how swollen it was. His left leg and right leg looked like they belonged to two different people.

He limped downstairs and found the ointment his dad left on the table, then hobbled into the bathroom to clean and rebandage the wound. Birk's stomach reminded him that he hadn't eaten much dinner, so he hopped around the kitchen gathering a bowl, spoon, dish towel, cereal, milk, and frozen peas.

While the frozen peas rested on this swollen leg, Birk wolfed down enough cereal to feed a small family. His stomach finally full and his leg feeling slightly better, he went outside to start on the trees. Ransom was immediately by his side.

Ransom sniffed at Birk's leg then looked up at him with his 'what have you done now' look.

"I know, I know. It was a stupid move. Let's get

you some fresh water and then you can help me stake up trees, okay?" Ransom wagged his tail in agreement.

There were two rows of Fraser fir saplings that Birk wanted to focus on. They were big enough to catch the wind and could snap off or get misshapen. He would stake them loosely—just enough to protect them from damage—but not so tight to prevent them from moving with the wind. Birk knew that the movement in the wind helped the trees grow stronger and he didn't want to interfere with that.

He had a bucket of wooden stakes in the barn that he would start with. If he needed more he could unstake some of the larger, more solid trees. This was a chore that he usually finished in a couple of hours, but his bum leg was slowing him down. Just walking to the barn was painful enough, and the work he usually did on his knees would have to be done bending over.

Birk had been struggling with the chore for some time when he saw his dad pull into the lane. He heard the truck door slam, and looked out of the corner of his eye to see him walk into the house. So Birk was surprised when his dad suddenly appeared by his side with two glasses of lemonade and a lawn chair.

"Here," Mick said, handing a glass to Birk. "Take a break. You're not doing that leg any favors."

Birk took a long drink of lemonade. "Thanks," he said, then to fill the awkward silence, "Is your truck fixed?"

"Yeah, it should keep running for another few months, anyway. How many more of these do you have to do?"

"I need to finish this row today. We're supposed to get thunderstorms with high winds tonight and tomorrow."

"Yeah, I heard that." Mick opened the lawn chair and settled it beside Birk. "Sit down and drink your lemonade. I'll finish out the row."

Birk plopped in the chair, relieved to be off his leg and grateful for the help.

~10~

A SPLENDID SATURDAY

Hannah kicked off her shoes and dipped her toes into the water. The cool sand felt good squishing between her toes. She slowly waded out until she was knee deep. The water was so refreshing, she had to restrain herself from diving under, cut-off shorts and all.

Her mom sat on a blanket nearby while her dad checked out the safety of the dock.

"Is it solid enough for everyone to walk on, Robert?" JoAnn asked.

"It's actually in pretty good shape. I think we'll go ahead and fish from here, so if you want to swim, we shouldn't get into each other's way."

"What'll it be Hannah? Fish or swim?" JoAnn asked.

"I want to do both, but I think I'll swim first. Jamie do you want to swim with me?" Hannah asked.

"I'm going to catch a fish first and then I'll swim," Jamie said.

"Oh, duh! I should have worn my swimsuit under my clothes. There's nowhere to change here," Hannah said.

"The car's unlocked, Hannah," Robert said. "Change in there. Maybe we should think about putting up a little cabin, something small with a deck or a covered porch looking out on the lake."

"Yeah!" Wes said. "A cabin would be so cool!"

"Then we could sleep over!" Jamie said.

"It *would* be nice to have a bathroom," JoAnn said.

"And a place to change!" Hannah shouted over her shoulder.

"Maybe right back there on that little knoll so we wouldn't need to worry about flooding," Robert said. "It could make a nice little family hideout for us."

"Then we'll have Hideout One and Hideout Two!" Jamie said.

Hannah changed into her swimsuit and ran for the lake. She didn't stop until she was deep enough for a shallow dive into the sparkling water. It was a tad on the chilly side, but Hannah didn't mind.

She swam a ways from shore and then stopped to tread water and look around. She saw nothing but trees to the right. A family of ducks swam behind a large boulder; a turtle pushed off from a log and plopped into the water. To her left, a good distance from their own dock, was a larger dock—*probably the public boat ramp.*

She could see a boat with two men off in the distance. Hannah flipped onto her back and floated. She closed her eyes and felt the sun warm her face.

The tranquility was suddenly interrupted with commotion from the dock. "Oh! Oh!" Jamie squealed.

"Jerk back on the pole, Jamie!" Robert said.

"I've got it! I've got it!"

Hannah flipped over to tread water and watch the show. She was reminded of the first time Jamie caught a fish on the Mississippi. He yanked so hard that the fish went flying through the air behind him and landed in a bucket.

"Easy now. Just reel it in," Robert said.

"I've got a bite, too!" Wes shouted.

Robert propped his pole into a knothole in one of the planks so he could help Jamie. Hannah thought she detected a wiggle on that pole, too.

"Dad! I think you have a bite!" Hannah warned him, laughing at the scene in front of her.

JoAnn jumped up from her blanket and ran to the dock to try to help.

Robert laughed. "This is a good problem to have!" He continued to help Jamie land his fish, while he looked over his shoulder at his wiggling pole. By now, everyone was laughing.

"I've got it!" JoAnn said, as she grabbed the pole and started to reel in the fish.

Hannah discovered that treading water and laughing weren't easy to do at the same time. She swam to shore and sat on the beach while the commotion continued.

"Look at that!" Robert said, holding up the stringer. "Three beauties! Looks like we'll have enough for a fish fry if we keep this up."

Jamie clapped his hands and announced, "I'm ready to swim now!"

JoAnn showed him how to open the car door and change behind it like a dressing room. Once changed, he ran for the beach and into the water, until Hannah yelled, "Jaime! Slow down! You don't know how to swim!"

"Oh yeah. Well, come and teach me."

Hannah held his hands while he kicked his legs. She showed him how to hold his breath and put his face in the water, blowing bubbles out his nose. She held on to him while she showed him how to kick his legs and move his arms to tread water. She held him by his stomach while he tried to float. She held onto his back, while he tried a back float.

After a time, he announced the lesson was over. "That's exhausting! I think I'll fish now."

Hannah laughed. "I think I did most of the work!"

"How about we all take a break and have some lunch?" JoAnn asked.

"And dessert!" Jamie answered.

They spread a blanket on the ground and ate like they hadn't eaten in days.

"I love it here, Poppa Bob," Jamie said.

"I'm glad, Jamie," Robert said. "I like it, too. I think I'm going to like it even better once you learn to swim. We need to get you signed up for lessons. Do they still give them at the Y, JoAnn?"

"I'm sure they do. I'll give them a call Monday," JoAnn said. "Can you swim, Wes?"

Wes smiled. "Like a fish! I'll show you after lunch."

They cleaned up from the picnic, put the fishing gear away and then all took a dip in the lake. Wes demonstrated that he was, indeed, a strong swimmer. JoAnn and Robert were assured that they only had to get lessons for Jamie.

The drive home was quiet. Hannah didn't really want to leave the lake, but she knew they would be back. She tried to take in everything about the McKenzie farm as they drove by. *Maybe there are other woods on the property that Birk was talking about.* She saw a dog on the porch and someone on the porch swing, but she couldn't be sure if it was Birk.

~11~

FEELING BETRAYED

Wheel Construction Inc. That's what the sign said on the side of the SUV that just went by the farm. Birk felt more betrayed than ever. His dad said he sold the property to a construction guy. But did it have to be Wheel Construction? Hannah and her brothers were adopted by a couple named Wheel. First his dad betrays him and now Hannah? Maybe. Probably. Unless there was more than one Wheel Construction in town. Not likely.

Birk left the porch swing and limped inside the house. His dad was at the kitchen table paying bills.

"Did Mr. Wheel buy the land?" Birk asked.

Birk had his answer as soon as he saw the expression on his dad's face. "What makes you think that?"

"His SUV just went by."

"That doesn't mean anything," Mick said.

"No, but your face does. I don't know why you don't just tell me. All I have to do is walk over there and ask them their name."

"Now, don't be bothering those people. They didn't take anything from you. *I* sold it. So if you're feeling the need to hate somebody, that would be me," Mick said.

Birk stared at the floor, feeling ashamed at his outburst from the night before. "I don't hate you."

"I know you don't, but you're mad at me and I understand. Maybe someday you'll understand why I felt it was necessary to do what I did. For now, understand that starting Monday I'm going to be gone from five in the morning until after dinner time. If your leg needs to be looked at by a doctor, it needs to happen today—now. I don't want to find you in the hospital with blood poisoning when I get home. So, you're going to let me look at it. Sit down."

He did seem to be feeling worse instead of better. Birk reluctantly plopped down into a chair and placed his leg in the empty chair between them. He grimaced in pain as he removed the bandages.

"Good grief, Birk. How in blazes did you manage this?" Mick looked up to find beads of sweat on Birk's brow.

"I kicked a stack of firewood and fell on a sharp stone."

Mick shook his head. "You've probably got tree bark and dirt in there." He put his hand on Birk's leg above and below the wound. "It's warmer than it should be. It's probably infected. Give Ransom fresh water and put some food in his dish. We'll likely be gone awhile."

* * *

Four hours and fifteen stitches later, Birk limped into the kitchen followed by his dad.

"Those shots the doctor gave you will be wearing off soon. He said you can take Tylenol if the pain gets bad. There's some in the medicine cabinet in the downstairs bathroom. At least they gave you something for the infection, so you won't likely lose your leg."

Birk rolled his eyes. He knew his dad was just trying to scare him. And though his leg didn't hurt right this second, he knew the urgent care bill was not in their budget and that did hurt. "I'm sorry about the doctor bill. You can take the money out of my college fund to pay for it."

"I'll accept your apology and trust you'll be more careful in the future. Whenever I got angry with your Grandpa Mac, I swept out the barn. Maybe try that next time." Mick started to put their carry-out order of fried chicken on plates.

"Can I eat mine upstairs?" Birk asked.

Mick didn't feel like arguing. He fixed his own plate and handed Birk the bag with the rest of the food.

Birk left the room and headed upstairs. Once in his room, he set the dinner aside and fired up his computer. Maybe his appetite would come back after he did a little homework. His bibliography was due Monday and he hadn't done any research on his paper. He was hoping to rely on his own family history for the source material, but Miss Barrett wanted more. *Do I even want to do this paper anymore?* Birk thought. The paper suddenly felt like one big lie. *Maybe he should give his notes to Hannah and she could write it since the land was hers now.*

If Birk was being honest with himself, he knew Hannah had nothing to do with buying the land. And though Birk wasn't ready to forgive Hannah's father, he knew he wasn't to blame either. Still, he was losing an important part of his family heritage and now it was theirs. It was hard not to be angry at everyone involved, but especially his dad.

At least they still had the Christmas tree farm. That's what he would write about. Besides, nearly everyone else in class was covering the river. He would stick with his plan.

Birk pulled up the outline he'd made for the paper. He was going to start with his Great-Great-Grandpa Cullen McKenzie coming over from Scotland in the early 1900s to purchase the land. He farmed and fished and raised sheep. Birk assumed he had cleared a lot of trees to make a place for his house and barn and the grazing sheep, but he didn't keep a record of all those details.

Cullen's son, Camdyn, took over the family farm, but only made occasional entries in the journals his father had begun. One thing he did note was the growth of white pines he and his father planted that still stood guard in front of the old forest. He didn't say why they planted them—maybe it reminded them of Scotland—but it was that stand of pines that gave Birk's Grandpa Mac the idea to start a Christmas tree farm.

Matthew McKenzie—Grandpa Mac—started small. First he planted a few trees to give to his neighbors for Christmas, but when interest took off, he turned it into a business. He hauled the cut trees to town to sell the weeks leading up to Christmas. Birk remembers helping his grandpa and his dad when he was very young. It was definitely Grandpa Mac that sparked an interest in trees for Birk. In fact, his grandpa even named him for a tree.

Birk's mother never made it home from the hospital after Birk was born. According to his grandpa, his father was too grief stricken over her death to be concerned about naming him, so Grandpa Mac took charge. Birk recalled the story his grandpa had told him years ago.

"Your mother moved here from the snowy north and her favorite tree was the birch. She loved how the white bark stood out against a forest of green. Birken is the Scottish word for birch and that's why you're called Birken McKenzie. I think she'd approve of finally having a birch on the land, don't you?"

Recalling the story made Birk smile, and he liked

that his name was unique. He didn't mind correcting people when they called him Bird, Bark, Kirk, or Dirk, either. Eventually, they got it.

Birk realized he was suddenly very hungry. He plunged into the bag of lukewarm chicken and French fries. It would have tasted better hot, but he wasn't about to go back downstairs to warm it up.

He ate while he gave more thought to his paper and his family history.

~12~

FEELING GUILTY

Hannah called Annie as soon as she got home. "Hi, Annie! We're home now and I still need to shower, but Mom said you could come over and have pizza with us, if you want. Then we can work on the school paper assignment."

"Oh, cool," Annie said. "Let me check."

"Oh, and tell your mom that we can pick you up and bring you home," Hannah said.

That clinched it. Annie's mom could keep playing with her new laptop undisturbed. "I'll be ready when you get here," Annie said.

* * *

Hannah and Annie took their pizza and drinks out on the balcony to eat. Hannah loved the little balcony that overlooked the courtyard where she and her brothers used to play when they were hiding from Olga. The courtyard was now transformed into a beautiful outdoor space that was Hannah's second favorite 'room' in their home--the first being her bedroom/artist studio.

"So how was the lake?" Annie asked.

"It's so beautiful there, Annie. We went swimming and the guys caught fish. Dad said we could build a small cabin on the property so we could sleep over sometimes. You *have* to come and stay with me when that happens."

"Shoot! I've got nothing against sleeping in a tent. I don't need the cabin, but, yeah, that'll be fun!"

That's one of the things Hannah loved about Annie. She loved the outdoors as much as Hannah and didn't mind roughing it in the name of fun.

"There's just one thing wrong with it, I think," Hannah hesitated.

"Poison ivy? Mosquitos? Snakes?" Annie smiled.

"Well, that's three things that could be wrong with it, but the big thing is that Dad bought the land from a nearby farmer. We passed a McKenzie mailbox right before we entered the property."

"You mean as in Birk McKenzie?" Annie asked, eyes wide.

"Yes, that McKenzie. The one that loves the land that has been in his family for over a hundred years."

"Ruh-roh," Annie said. "You think he'll find out and hate you?"

"I don't want him to hate me, true, but mostly I don't want my family's good fortune to be the reason for his unhappiness."

"You don't know for sure that it's his land or that he's unhappy about it, right?" Annie asked.

"Dad bought it from a McKenzie. I don't know for certain if Birk is unhappy about it. I can only guess."

"Then let's hope for the best. Don't worry about a problem that may not even exist."

"You're right. Thanks, Annie. I knew talking to you would help. Okay, I'm going to grab us a couple more pieces of pizza. Here's a list Dad came up with for places we could call on for the school paper ads. See what you think and what you might want to add."

* * *

When it was time for Annie to go home, Robert offered to drive her. "I need to run into Paper Clips for some lead and drafting paper to work on the cabin design. Anybody need anything?"

"Magnifying glass!" Jamie called.

"What's that for, Jamie?" Robert asked.

"If you're having trouble seeing, then maybe you need glasses," JoAnn added.

"I can see fine, but detectives use them to look for clues."

Hannah covered her mouth to stifle a snicker. Annie gave her a quizzical look. "He's been reading my

Nancy Drew mysteries," Hannah explained.

"Ah. So you're a detective now, Jamie?" Annie asked.

"Yes, but I need a good mystery. Do you have one you'd like me to solve?" Jamie said.

"Not right now, but I'll let you know if one comes up."

"Okay, girls. Let's go," Robert said. "There's a magnifying glass in the center drawer of my desk, Jamie. You're welcome to use it, but be careful with it and return it when you're done."

"Thank you for picking me up and for the pizza, Mrs. Wheel!" Annie said.

"Any time, Annie," JoAnn said.

"Oh wait, I don't have my notebook," Annie said. "Where did I put that?"

"I know!" Jamie said, as he ran out to the balcony. "Here it is. You left it on the table outside."

"Thank you, Jamie! You know, I don't think you really need that magnifying glass," Annie said, smiling.

After dropping off Annie and hitting the Paper Clip store, Hannah joined her dad in the front seat. "Hey, Dad, do you know the McKenzie man that you bought the land from?"

"I don't know him personally, but I know who you mean, yes," Robert glanced at Hannah, then pulled out into traffic.

"Well, you said that he is probably Birk's dad. Do you know that for certain?"

"Not for certain, no, but I've seen a map of the nearby property owners. I bought it from the farmer who has the Christmas tree farm."

"Did the map show any other forest on their land?" Hannah asked.

"Not that I recall—just the trees from the Christmas tree farm and the few that are around their house."

Hannah's shoulders sagged. She turned her head and stared out the side window.

"Why does that bother you, Hannah?"

"Birk is doing his English paper on his farm. He told us that his great-great-grandfather came over from Scotland, bought the land and planted a pine forest. It's been in his family for over a hundred years. I don't think he would want his dad to sell it."

"Hmmm. I didn't ask why he was selling it, but I figured they no longer wanted it, or at least wanted the money more. The realtor did say that the seller wanted to know how I would be using the land. I shared with him that we would be using it for our family to fish and swim. Maybe he was afraid I would start cutting down trees and putting up condos or something, though he was being pretty trusting to take my word for it."

Hannah had a panicked look on her face. "You wouldn't *ever*, would you?"

"No, Hannah. The land is just for our use and our friends—your friends. I don't have any interest in removing the natural privacy that the woods provide. That's a big part of the charm, don't you agree?"

"Yes. I wouldn't want to change anything about it," Hannah said. A hint of a smile passed her lips. "Except to add a cabin."

Robert smiled back. "We agree. Feel free to let your friend know our plans and let him know he's welcome over any time."

Hannah wondered how that would go over. *You're welcome to visit us on your land any time, Birk.*

~13~

THE MCKENZIE TREES

It was still dark when Birk heard his dad leave for work. He glanced at the clock on his nightstand. *Ugh, it was only five.* Another two and half hours before the bus would be there. He closed his eyes and tried to go back to sleep, but it was useless. He switched on the light and looked down at his leg. The swelling had gone down, but the bruise was huge and almost black. At least it wasn't throbbing anymore and he would be wearing jeans to school so nobody would see it.

Birk got dressed and went downstairs. Ransom greeted him at the bottom, tail wagging.

"Hey, boy. What are you doing inside?" Birk sat on the bottom steps to give Ransom a proper greeting. "I guess Dad thought you could keep me company, huh? Well, let's get you something to drink."

Ransom barked his approval and ran to the pantry door.

"Oh. You need a treat, too, huh?"

Birk switched on the kitchen light and saw a note on the table from his dad, along with a note signed by the urgent care doctor.

"Good. I don't have to go to PE class. I really don't feel like putting on shorts or running laps. Just so you know, Ransom, Dad says you need to go back outside when I leave for school but you can come inside at night. What'dya think about that? It isn't even winter yet and you get to be a house dog again." Birk scratched Ransom behind his ears. "My four-legged babysitter."

Birk gave Ransom his water and treat then ate his own breakfast. By the time he cleaned up the dishes, dawn was shedding enough light on the farm to let him check his trees. He needed to make sure the stakes held in last night's storm and no damage had been done.

Birk put on his mud boots, grabbed a jacket and went outside. Ransom followed. A walk through the staked saplings confirmed that the winds had been high and the rain plentiful.

A few of the stakes Birk had put in the ground in his handicapped state were now sitting at an angle or lying on the ground. Fortunately, no trees appeared damaged. Birk left the stakes as is so he could find them after school to pound them in better. The ground needed to dry out a little first. He walked over to the older trees—the ones that would be ready to sell at harvest.

There were at least two hundred trees ready to sell—most were eight years old but some younger. They grew at different speeds depending on the variety. They all looked pretty good shape-wise. Every year, each tree had to be pruned to make sure they had a single leader stem and to make sure they all had a nice cone shape. Birk was allowed to assist with the smaller trees, but they hired help so they could get through all their stock within the prime two weeks each summer.

Birk needed to talk to his dad about getting the plastic balers ordered. They normally hired a few high school guys to help with the cutting, baling, loading, and set-up. That and the truck rental could wait until closer to Thanksgiving, but he would need to lock down the rental location.

Last year they rented the Memorial Auditorium parking lot. As long as there were no shows scheduled for the Friday after Thanksgiving and the weekends following, that would be the best place. He would ask his dad to make the phone call to get it booked.

"Come on, boy. Let's get the bird feed and take a walk." Birk went back to the house to get the bucket of feed. He knew it wasn't his land anymore, but nobody would be there this time of day. He grabbed his pocketknife, too. There was one final piece of business he needed to tend to.

* * *

The circle of trees had done a good job of protecting the clearing from the previous night's thunderstorm. The only real mess was due to Birk's 'storm' from three days ago. He filled the bird feeder, straightened up the stones he had kicked from the fire pit, and restacked the kicked logs. The wind chime was a tangled mess. He would work on that later.

This had been a special place for Birk and his Grandpa Mac. Clearly, it had been special to the generations before them, too. Maybe it wasn't really his anymore, but he would always feel a connection. He walked over to the towering pine with the patch of missing bark. He felt the carvings of each of the names that were part of the McKenzie family. He took out his pocketknife and carved one more.

~14~

A NEED TO KNOW

Hannah anxiously took her seat in Miss Barrett's class. She kept her eye on the door aware of everyone who entered. She was watching for Birk. If he smiled at her as he normally did, then everything was okay. Or maybe that just meant he didn't know about the land being sold. At least that would mean things were okay for the day. But if he didn't smile, then it would be a bad sign. Hannah could feel her heart pounding in her throat.

Birk was the last student to enter the class and he was limping.

"Are you okay, Birk?" Miss Barrett asked.

"Yeah, I'm fine. Just a minor injury."

Hannah glanced at his leg to see if he was in a cast. He wasn't and he wasn't looking at her, either. The entire walk to his desk he looked straight ahead. He didn't look at her when he sat down, either.

Maybe he looked at me when I was looking at his leg. Maybe he's just embarrassed that he is limping and doesn't want anyone to look at him. Or maybe he never looked at me because he hates me. Hannah didn't know what to think, but she knew she couldn't keep staring at him, hoping for a reaction. She needed to accept the fact that Birk may not want to be friends anymore. Hannah looked toward the front of the room. Annie turned around in her chair and gave her a sympathetic shrug. *So Annie saw it, too.*

Not one to leave things alone, Annie leaned out of her seat and turned toward Birk. "Pssst, Birk. What'd you do to your leg?" she whispered.

"I tripped and fell on a pile of stones. Had to get stitches," he answered, then got busy shuffling his books. He never looked at Hannah.

"Ouch!" Annie said. "Get better."

Birk gave his head a half nod without looking at Annie.

Hannah did her best to focus on school and tried to forget about Birk, but when lunch time rolled around, she couldn't find Annie fast enough. She plopped down beside her and pulled her lunch from her back-pack.

"No school lunch today?" Annie asked.

"No. I don't like the ham salad so I brought pea-nut butter and jelly. Want some?" Hannah held out half of her sandwich.

"No, I'm good. Thanks." Annie opened her mouth to bite into her ham salad.

"Well, now we know. He hates me, doesn't he?" Hannah said.

Annie closed her mouth and put her sandwich down. "Hannah, nobody could hate you. But something's up, for sure. Maybe he was just hurting from his leg. Or maybe he's mad at his dad and he's just going to take it out on everyone for a while. Just give him time."

"He didn't take it out on you," Hannah said.

"I spoke to *him*, Hannah, so he had to answer. He wasn't exactly Mr. Friendly when he responded. Just go up to him and talk to him." Annie said.

Hannah knew she was right. She just needed to go up to Birk and see what's what. If he knows about the land, and he probably does, there is no point in pretending. They needed to talk about it and move on, if they were going to stay friends.

Hannah had one more class with Birk—science—and it was the last class of the day. They didn't sit together, but she would talk to him right after. She just needed to figure out what to say.

By the time the bell rang, she still hadn't figured it out. She gathered up her books and shoved them into her bag, all the while practicing her ice breaker. *Hey, Birk, how was your weekend, other than hurting your leg and losing your land? No. Hi, Birk. It seemed you couldn't stand to look at me in English class. Any special reason why? No. Hi, Birk. Did you hear? My dad bought part of your family's land. Would you like to visit it sometime? No.*

Hannah was in the hall now and saw Birk limping

ahead of her. It was now or never. She quickened her step until she was walking next to him. He glanced at her, but then looked forward and kept walking.

"Birk," was all she said.

"Yeah?" He glanced at her, but didn't smile.

"Are you okay?" Hannah couldn't believe how lame she sounded.

He stopped walking and turned toward her--still not smiling. "Why wouldn't I be okay, Hannah?"

"Well, I don't know but it seemed like you—,"

"You probably thought I wouldn't be happy that my dad sold off the best part of our land to your dad so you and your rich family would have a nice place to play on the weekends. Is that it?"

Hannah felt her face burn and her eyes start to sting. "I didn't know he was going—."

"Forget it. It's no big deal. I've gotta catch the bus." Birk took off and didn't give Hannah another look.

Hannah could feel her chin start to quiver. She walked to her locker with her head down, trying to re-gain control. She pulled out the books she would need for homework and put the others away. Soon Wes and Jamie were standing by her.

"Why's your face all red, Hannah?" Jamie asked.

Hannah shook her head.

"Are you embarrassed or mad or what?" Jamie asked.

Hannah ignored him.

Wes glanced at Hannah. "Just leave her alone, Jamie. She's upset and you're making it worse. Let's go find Mom."

The three walked outside, right past the lineup of kids waiting for bus number three. Wes waved and called out to his friend. "Hey, Dillon!"

"Hey, Wes! See you tomorrow!"

Hannah and Jamie glanced over to see who Dillon was. He was standing right next to Birk. Birk looked at Hannah and then looked at the ground. Hannah quickly looked away.

"I saw that!" Jamie said, "And your face is red again. Mystery solved!"

Wes looked at Hannah with a puzzled expression.

"You don't know what you're talking about, Jamie," Hannah hissed.

"It's something to do with Dillon or Birk, isn't it?" Jamie asked.

"I don't even know Dillon!" Hannah said, soon realizing her mistake.

“Birk then,” Jamie said, smiling.

“Jamie, quit being a jerk,” Wes said. “Hey, there’s Mom.”

Hannah couldn’t get to the car fast enough.

~15~

REGRETS

Dillon started jabbering as soon as he spotted Birk waiting for the after school bus. "I thought you were walking kinda funny when we got off the bus this morning. You're really limping now. What'd you do, anyway?"

"I had a fight with a stack of wood and had to get stitches," Birk explained.

"No way! How many stitches?" Dillon asked.

"Fifteen. How was camping?"

"Oh, it was pretty cool. I didn't have to babysit much. We fished and kayaked and went swimming. It was pretty fun, until it started to rain. Did you get everything worked out with your dad?"

Birk snorted. "I wouldn't call it worked out. You were right about the seedlings. We're not ordering this year. He isn't working at Flinthills Cabinets anymore and has a long drive to his new job so won't be around as much."

"Yeah, he asked Dad to keep an eye on you," Dillon said.

"I don't need a babysitter."

"I don't think he means like that, but you can come over and have dinner with us sometime. Hey, you could spend the night!"

Birk shrugged and gave Dillon a half smile.

"Or just call if you need anything," Dillon said.

Birk nodded. "Thanks." He didn't feel like telling Dillon about the land, so kept that piece of news to himself. "Hey, how do you know that Wes kid you said 'hi' to?"

"We have a couple classes together and we're both in chess club," Dillon said. He glanced at Birk and shifted nervously in the seat. "He said he drove by our farm Saturday on the way to some land that his dad bought."

Birk looked down at the backpack he had on the bus floor between his knees. He tightened his grip on the handle and glanced at Dillon. *He probably knows about the land.* Birk didn't trust himself to speak, so just nodded his head. Dillon had a pretty good idea what the land and its history meant to Birk.

When the bus finally stopped at Dillon's house, he grabbed his backpack to leave, but turned to Birk and mumbled "Sorry, Birk," then scurried off the bus.

Yep, he knows. Birk released the breath he'd been holding and slumped back into the seat.

* * *

Ransom ran to greet Birk. He got a quick scratch behind the ear as they walked to the house together. Birk changed out of his school clothes, filled Ransom's food and water dishes and then went out to the field to fix the stakes that the storm had messed up. The ground wasn't muddy anymore, but still soft enough to make it easy to drive the stakes.

Birk put his tools away when he finished then picked some ripened tomatoes, potatoes and carrots from the vegetable garden. Maybe they could have BLTs for dinner. Birk fixed a snack and then sat at the kitchen table to do his homework, Ransom at his side.

He had been staring at his history book for fifteen minutes reading the same page over and over but not absorbing anything he'd read. *Maybe you can't focus because you were a jerk to Hannah,* he thought. His conversation with Hannah kept playing over and over in his mind. *It wasn't even a conversation—it was just you being a stupid fool.*

Why did he have to throw in that *your rich family*? *That was just plain lame.* He didn't care if her parents had money. He was happy for her. She'd had a rough couple of years in her life and she deserved happiness. He couldn't even blame her dad for buying the land. He didn't steal it from them. Birk's dad listed it for sale and that was that.

Birk thought about calling Hannah to apologize. He didn't like the idea of being responsible for upsetting her. Maybe she would hang up on him, but he needed to try. He didn't have her number. In fact, he didn't have any girl's number. He didn't know if she had a cell phone or a land line, but he figured her dad probably had a land line for his construction business. Birk limped up the stairs to get on the computer to search for the Wheel Construction phone number. He took a deep breath and dialed the number before he had time to change his mind.

"Wheel Construction. Robert speaking."

"Uh. Hello. This is Birk McKenzie. I'm a friend, er, classmate of Hannah's. Can I talk to her at this number?"

"Oh, hi, Birk. This is the business phone, but I can give you the home number. Ready?"

Birk grabbed a pencil and paper. "Yes, ready." Mr. Wheel gave Birk the phone number. "Thanks, Mr. Wheel. Bye."

Birk sagged in his chair, suddenly nervous about making the call. "Come on, Ransom. Let's boil the potatoes so they're ready to fry when Dad gets home."

~16~

GIVE IT TIME

Hannah went to her room as soon as she got home, shut the door and plopped face down on the bed. The tears she had been fighting gushed onto her pillow. *She was never going to speak to Birk McKenzie again! She was wrong to think he was a nice guy. He was just plain mean!*

Hannah heard a light tapping on her door. She curled into a ball on her side and wiped her eyes.

"Go away, Jamie."

"Is everything okay, Hannah?" her Mom asked.

"Oh. Yeah, it's fine."

The door slowly opened. "And yet, you don't sound fine. You were very quiet on the drive home."

Hannah's chin started to quiver again.

"Can you tell me what's bothering you, sweetie?"

Hannah shook her head.

"Your detective brother is sure it has something to do with either Dillon or Birk." JoAnn grinned. "I don't know where he comes up with these ideas."

"It's Birk!" Hannah sobbed, burying her head in her pillow.

"Oh, okay. Oh! Is it about the land?" JoAnn asked.

"Yes! He's mad at me for it and there's nothing I can do." A new batch of tears streamed down Hannah's face.

"Hannah, he's going to realize that this has nothing to do with you. He's probably just hurt that his dad sold the land and so he's striking out. He'll come to his senses. You know, if your dad realized this was going to cause you problems, he wouldn't have bought the land. I would talk to him about it, but I'm guessing Birk's dad must need the money."

Hannah wiped her face. "No, don't talk to him about it. Dad said he isn't going to cut down any trees. If he sells the land to somebody else, they might. It's okay. It's just, Birk's not the friend I thought he was."

"He needs some time, Hannah. Why don't you wash your face and come out to the kitchen so we can get started on your school ad? I'll fix you a cup of hot tea while you think up something catchy, okay?"

"Okay, Mom. And thanks." Hannah sat up and gave her Mom a hug.

JoAnn started out the door, but turned around. "Do you sometimes wonder if Jamie might make a good detective after all?"

Hannah laughed. "Yes, but he doesn't have to be

so annoying about it!"

* * *

"Have the police found Olga, yet, Poppa Bob?" Jamie asked at dinner.

"No. They said they usually put a trace on credit cards or debit cards to find where a fugitive is headed, but Olga didn't use either, so she's going to be harder to find. They also checked the airlines and trains to see if she bought a ticket, but no hits there, either.

"In the meantime, the city has approved using the house for a homeless shelter. Sometime in the next week or so we need to go over there and see if there's anything you kids may have left behind that you want to save.

"I think everything we had was taken to your thrift shop and you returned all of that to us," Wes said.

"Wait!" Hannah said with widening eyes. "My bracelet!"

"Oh, yeah!" Jamie said.

"What bracelet is that?" JoAnn asked.

Hannah told her the story about Aunt Olga ripping her bracelet off her wrist when she tried to sneak a little hot water into Jamie's bath. "I tried looking for it when I would dust or clean her room, but I never found it. It was the bracelet Mom and Dad gave me for my seventh birthday."

"That woman!" JoAnn said, shaking her head. She reached out and squeezed Hannah's hand.

"If it's there, we'll find it, Hannah," Robert said.

"Whoa, not so fast everybody," Jamie said. "This sounds like a mystery to me."

"We have to remember that she may have taken it with her or even sold it," Robert said.

Jamie thought for a moment, then shook his head. "I don't think so," he said.

"Why do you say that?" Hannah asked.

"Oh, sorry to interrupt, Hannah, but did Birk McKenzie call you?" Robert asked.

Hannah thought she was hearing things. "What? No. Why would you ask me that?"

"Why would you ask her that?" JoAnn repeated.

Robert looked from Hannah to JoAnn. "Whoa. Easy. He called me at work to ask for you so I gave him the home phone number. Should I not have done that? I thought you were friends."

"How long ago?" Hannah asked, her face starting to flush.

Jamie smiled, pointing at Hannah's face. "Uh, Hannah? Your face is turning really..."

"I know, Jamie!" Hannah blurted. "Don't you think I can feel it for myself?"

Jamie shrugged.

Robert glanced at his watch."He called me about three hours ago."

Hannah looked at her Mom and shrugged.

"That's something, anyway," JoAnn said. "Just give him time."

"So!" Jamie said. "I'm guessing he's your boy-friend, right?"

"No!" Hannah was quick to respond. "He's a friend. He was a friend. He's a classmate."

Just then the phone rang. Hannah jumped.

"I'll get it!" Jamie shouted and ran for the phone.

"Oh great," Hannah said. "Can we ban him from answering the phone, *please*?"

"Hannah, it's your boyfriend!" Jamie called out with way too much volume.

"Oh my gosh! See what I mean?" Hannah didn't know if she should be embarrassed or excited. She decided she was both.

~17~

LIFTING WEIGHTS

Birk's dad walked in the door after seven, his step slow, his eyes tired. Birk had decided to fix the BLTs and potatoes without waiting for him, so they could sit down to eat as soon as he got home. It was a good call.

"Mmm. It smells good in here. Thanks for fixing dinner, Birk. That drive makes for a long day."

"How did it go?" Birk asked.

Mick gave Birk a quick glance, then went to the sink to wash his hands. "Good and bad, I guess. They've decided I'm skilled enough they want me to go on extended hours."

"What? You were gone eleven hours today. They want you to work longer?"

They both sat at the table to eat.

"I know, but I can't blame them for my long drive. I don't like it, but I don't feel like I can refuse when I've just been hired. Besides, we can use the extra money. I know this isn't fair to you. I have the option of working the weekend rather than adding the extra hours to each day. Do you have a preference?"

"So then you would get no days off? You wouldn't like that, Dad."

"It's temporary, but we'll see. Maybe I could work an extra two hours a day and then just work Saturday instead of both Saturday and Sunday."

"Why don't you advertise your wood working, Dad? If people saw the tables and dressers and chairs you've made, they would be standing in line to place orders."

Mick chuckled. "Thanks for the vote of confidence, son, but making furniture is slow business unless I have a crew. Even then, I would be footing the bill for health insurance and other expenses that would take a big chunk of the profits."

Birk felt bad for his dad and a little sorry for himself. He basically would be seeing his dad after dinner or on Sundays. Other than that, it would be him and Ransom. Alone.

"I've talked to Dillon's dad, Birk, and they are fine with you having dinner with them and staying there until I get home. I can pick you up on my way home so you wouldn't need to spend the night, but I would feel a lot better knowing you were with them. It's too long for a twelve-year-old to be alone."

"If I need anything, I'll call them. I'll be fine here. I have Ransom."

"I figured you'd say that. Well, don't wait for me for dinner from now on. You go ahead and eat without me and I'll fix mine when I get home. I'm going to shower and then I'll clean up the dishes."

"My homework's done. I'll do the dishes, Dad."

Birk felt like a weight was on his shoulders. First the land getting sold, then his dad's job, the fight with Hannah, and now the news about his dad's extra hours. Hannah. Was he going to call her or not? He knew he would feel better if he could patch things up with her—remove some of the weight he was feeling. He picked up the phone and dialed the number Robert had given him.

A little kid answered. "Hello?"

"Hi. This is Birk McKenzie. Is Hannah there?"

"Hang on." Birk had to pull the phone from his ear when he heard a loud "Hannah! It's your boyfriend!"

Jish, Birk thought. *There are definite benefits to being an only child!*

"Hello?" Hannah said.

"Hi, Hannah. This is Birk."

"Hi, Birk. Sorry about my annoying little brother."

Birk chuckled, relieved that Hannah didn't hang up on him. "That's okay. He's kinda loud, huh?" Birk cleared his throat, "Hey, Hannah? I'm sorry I was a jerk to you today. I didn't mean it. You were being nice and I was a creep. I wish I could take it all back."

"That's okay. I know you're upset about the land. When Dad told us about it, I didn't know it was yours. He didn't know it was yours or what it means to you." Hannah lowered her voice to a whisper. "I'm sorry it got sold."

"Well, you didn't have anything to do with it and I don't blame your dad, either. He didn't steal it, he bought it fair and square. I was outta line. So, friends?"

"Yes. Friends…and, Birk?"

"Yeah?"

"He isn't going to cut down any of the trees. He told me and I believe him. He loves the trees, too."

Birk could only nod, his words stuck in his throat.

"Thanks for calling me, Birk. I'll see you tomorrow."

Birk nodded again, then hung up the phone. He plopped down onto the closest chair. Two huge weights were lifted from his shoulders: his friendship with Hannah was safe, and the trees were, too.

~18~

MAKING PLANS

The rest of the week sped by for Hannah. She and Annie turned in payments and two pages of ads for the school paper. Mr. Galvin was pleased with what they had accomplished and very complimentary of Hannah's art-work on the bakery ad.

The deadline for her English paper was a week away. She had finished her notes and outline; now she just needed to start writing it. She had already drawn a page of crinoid pictures to accompany her paper. That was the easy part.

It was a relief to be on friendly terms with Birk again. Her school days wouldn't be the same without his ready smile and kind words. Annie was all ears when Hannah told her about their fight and Birk's apology.

"Wow! All this drama and I missed it! And he *called* you? Has he ever called you before?" Annie lifted her right eyebrow in that way that always made Hannah laugh.

"You goofball" Hannah laughed. "Lower that brow because, no, he's never called me before. He just called to apologize. It's no big deal. I mean. I'm glad he did."

"The cutest guy in sixth grade called you, Hannah," Annie teased. "It's a pretty big deal. Anyway, I'm glad things are good with you, so maybe we can talk about something else, now? Like, are you going trick-or-treating this year? I mean, you have to go. So, what are you going as?"

Hannah laughed. "I haven't really thought about it, but I guess that's coming up in a few weeks, huh? We'll need to take my little brother, probably, but I'll dress up for sure. I just don't know what I'll be yet."

"Well, I've thought about mine already," Annie said. "I'm going to look authentically witchy!"

"Ooh! Witches are my favorite, too," Hannah said. "But I lived with one for two years, so I think I'll try something different." Hannah realized that she hadn't gone trick-or-treating for three years in a row. The last time she went, she was in third grade. Some people may think she was a little old to be going now, but it had always been fun and she wanted to go again.

It wasn't the 'treat' part that she liked the best, although that was probably more important when she was smaller. She loved being outside on a cool October night with the moon glowing through the trees, leaves rustling and falling all around and the streets full of kids in all manner of strange and funny costumes. She didn't want to miss that magical night.

* * *

Jamie had started his swimming lessons and was learning fast. He had no problem putting his head under water, but needed more practice with his arm movements. Robert suggested they go to the lake on Saturday so Jamie could show off his moves and he could work on staking out where the cabin would go. It would likely be their last chance to swim in the lake before temperatures got too cool.

"That sounds like a good idea to me," JoAnn said. "Everybody agree?"

Hannah, Wes and Jamie all agreed. Now that Hannah knew Birk wasn't angry at them for owning the land, she was anxious to go back. This time she wanted to explore the woods a little.

"Okay, that's settled," Robert said. "By the way, I took Denny over to Olga's old house to look around." Denny was Robert's crew foreman and sometimes fishing buddy. "The city doesn't want any of the furniture, but Denny's church is having a huge give-away. He said he could empty the house for us. I would like you kids to have a look through everything before he does that. At least you and Wes, Hannah. Are you up for going over there Sunday afternoon?"

"Sure," Hannah said. "I want to check the desk for my bracelet."

"Yeah, I'll help," Wes said.

"I think I'll stay here with Momma Jo," Jamie said. "Unless you need me?"

"We can handle it, Jamie," Hannah said. "By the way, last week you said you were pretty sure Olga didn't take my bracelet with her. Why did you say that?"

Jamie shrugged. "You know what she looked like. She never fixed herself up and she sure didn't wear jewelry, so you know she didn't take it to wear. It wouldn't fit her, anyway, except maybe her big toe. It was a pretty bracelet, but it wasn't diamonds or anything, right?"

"Right," Hannah answered. "It was my birthstone, garnets."

Jamie continued. "So she wouldn't try to sell it, I don't think. If she were going to trade it for something, she would have taken it to the Wheel and Deal Thrift Shop like she did our other things, but she didn't do that or Momma Jo or Curtis would have told us."

"She didn't bring in a bracelet when I saw her and Curtis wouldn't have allowed her back in the shop," JoAnn said.

Jamie nodded. "I think she took it from you and hid it just to be mean and she probably forgot about it after we ran away. So, it's still in the house. Yeah. For sure. It's in the house."

The room went silent.

"Uh, why's everyone staring at me like that?"

Jamie asked.

"We're trying to figure out how someone so young can be so clever!" JoAnn said.

"Seriously, dude," Wes said. "Maybe you *are* the next Nancy Drew."

Jamie liked the sounds of that. "Jamie Drew-Faris-Wheel, Master Sleuth at your service!"

"I just hope you're right, Jamie," Hannah said.

~19~

UNSTITCHED

The stitches on Birk's leg were getting tight and itchy. With his dad working Monday through Saturday, he figured he was on his own to get them taken out. The urgent care doctor said he could return in seven to ten days to get them pulled and he wouldn't need an appointment.

To get there he would need to take the city bus to the urgent care center after school and then wouldn't have a ride home. He could ask Boone to take him, but he told his dad he could handle things on his own so he decided he would.

Birk powered up the PC and did a search on removing stitches at home. "It looks easy, Ransom. I just need tweezers, small scissors, rubbing alcohol, and a couple bandages. Piece of cake!"

Ransom whined.

"If it starts bleeding, I'll stop, okay?" Ransom followed Birk to the bathroom to watch him get the necessary supplies.

Birk poured some of the rubbing alcohol on the scissors and tweezers and then poured some on a cotton ball to clean off the wound. Carrying his supplies into the living room, he sat on the sofa to complete the task.

"Here goes nothing." He used the tweezers to gently lift the knot of the first stitch. He wedged the scissors under the knot and snipped. He stopped. He looked up at the ceiling and took a deep breath. He slowly tugged the stitch through his leg. "Eeew. That feels creepy."

Ransom whined.

Birk took another deep breath, then shook his hands in the air, trying to ease his nerves. "Don't worry. It doesn't hurt. It just feels weird." He swiped the beads of sweat from his forehead and finished removing all fifteen stitches. Once done, he dabbed rubbing alcohol on the wound again. He blew on his leg until the alcohol dried, applied the two bandages, then fell back into the sofa.

Ransom rested his nose on Birk's knee. "I'm fine. Just give me a minute, then we'll go mow before it gets too warm."

* * *

Even though they had a riding mower, they had a lot of lawn to mow. It was nearly lunch time when Birk finished and put the mower in the barn. If he hadn't just taken out his stitches, he would have walked to the lake for a swim, but decided a shower would be safer. He glanced at the bandaged injury. Still no blood. *Good!*

He fixed a sandwich from left-over meatloaf, grabbed an apple and a thermos of milk, then packed them into his backpack. He put a couple treats in his pocket for Ransom, grabbed the bucket of bird feed and headed out the door.

"Come on, Ransom. Let's go visit the McKenzie trees."

Birk stopped in the barn to get a length of fishing line and some wire cutters. He stuck them in his pocket and continued through the woods. He took a deep breath and smiled. He loved the smell of freshly cut grass mixed with the clean pine smell from the trees.

He was going to have lunch in the clearing today. He knew it wasn't his anymore, but he was pretty sure he wouldn't be kicked out. He did his best thinking there, and he needed to do some thinking.

Birk bent down to pick up a stick and threw it deep into the woods. Ransom had it recovered in seconds and returned to Birk's side for a redo. "Good boy! Now see if you can find this one!" Birk threw it deeper into the woods, not sure where it landed. But Ransom was on the run while it was still airborne and found it in no time. Birk chuckled. "I swear you're smiling right now. Okay, one more throw all the way to the clearing."

Birk felt an immediate sense of calm when he stepped through the trees. He took the stick from Ransom and laid it on top of the pile of firewood.

"Later, boy. Let's feed these hungry birds." Birk took a treat from his pocket. "Now sit and behave, okay?"

Birk filled the empty feeder. He gathered up all the parts of the broken wind chime, pulled the fishing line and cutters from his pocket and started making repairs. He tied the last knot and pulled on it to make sure it would hold. Ransom suddenly stood up and looked towards the path that meandered through the native woods. Birk stopped working and listened.

He heard car doors slamming and the murmur of distant voices.

Ransom gave a short bark.

"Hush,." Birk commanded. "Sit!"

Ransom looked at Birk and whined.

"It's okay. Sit." Birk pulled another treat from his pocket and rewarded Ransom for resisting the urge to chase down Hannah's family. The growth of trees around Birk's clearing was too thick for him to see anyone, but that also meant they couldn't see him. He sat down on the moss covered log and took his lunch out of his backpack. He listened to his neighbors between bites and gulps of milk.

Birk was certain the voices were coming from the clearing by the lake. Another reason why it was a smart move for Birk to skip swimming today. He washed down his sandwich with a long drink of milk, then reached for the apple.

"Why are you looking at me with those puppy dog eyes? You think they're having more fun than us?"

Ransom stood up and barked.

Birk laughed and patted the log. "Come here, boy!" Ransom looked back at Birk. "I'll share my apple with you." But Ransom suddenly sprang forward and started wagging his tail. Birk got up and reached for Ransom's collar just as Hannah pushed her way through the trees.

~20~

A VISIT TO THE CLEARING

Hannah nearly fell backwards from surprise. "Birk!" she said.

"Hi, Hannah." Birk held tightly onto his dog's collar.

"Sorry, I didn't mean to—."

"It's okay," Birk said. "I'm the one that should apologize. I'm on your land."

Hannah's ears felt warm. She knew her face was turning red. *This was so awkward.* To hide her embarrassment, she started looking all around her. It was so serene—so perfect.

She stood inside a circle of evergreen trees on a pile of cushy pine needles. A fire pit in the center of the clearing was neatly lined and bordered with stones. Firewood was stacked nearby. A large bird feeder hung from a branch, filled with bird feed. Even the moss-covered log looked like it was intentionally placed there for a comfortable place to sit.

"No," Hannah said. "This is clearly yours. It's beautiful. Did you do all this?"

Birk's dog seemed eager to break free.

"Easy, Ransom. It was mostly Mother Nature, with the help of my ancestors, I guess. I've added a few things. I know it's yours now, but I hoped you wouldn't mind if I visited now and then. I put out feed for the birds and I was fixing this." Birk held up the wind chimes he had been repairing.

"Is it okay if I pet him? Ransom, did you say?"

"Sure. He may lick you to death, but he won't bite."

"He's beautiful." Hannah squatted down and scratched Ransom behind the ears. He thanked her by rubbing his neck against her and licking her face. Hannah laughed. "Is that wind chimes you're holding?"

"Yeah, I just made them out of some old stuff I found lying around. It got caught in a storm and kinda fell apart."

"This place seems like it would be really well protected from any storms," Hannah said.

Birk shrugged. "From most storms, yeah. Here, you wanna sit down?" Birk waved at the empty log.

"Sure. I can't stay long. I told Dad I wanted to go for a quick walk before lunch. There's a pretty clear path through those trees. I just followed that so I could find my way back. I can see why you love it here so much."

Hannah looked all around her and up at the tops of the trees where dappled sun light filtered through. She spotted a carving on a nearby tree. She stood and walked over for a closer look.

"Cullen, Camdyn, Matthew, Michael…," she read.

"Michael is my dad, but everyone calls him Mick," Birk explained. He joined Hannah at the tree. "And that's my Grandpa Mac, Great-Grandpa Camdyn, and Great- Great-Grandpa Cullen was the first one here."

Hannah pointed to the final name on the list, the one that was freshly carved. "And Birken? Is that your real name?"

"Yeah. It's Scottish for birch. That was my mom's favorite tree, I guess. She died when I was born, so I never knew her."

"Wow. That must be hard. I lost my real mom, too. And my dad, but at least I knew them so I have something to remember."

"I heard about that. Sorry that happened to you, and that whole business with your aunt. She sounds like a real piece of work."

"Good old Aunt Olga. We always called her Aunt Ogre behind her back."

Birk laughed. "Good one!"

"She was supposed to be in court this week for child abuse charges, but they can't find her. They think she left town. Probably left Iowa, too."

"Seriously?" Birk said. "Well, hopefully, she never comes back."

"That would be fine with me! My brothers, too. Well, I should probably get back." Hannah's face suddenly lit up. "Hey, would you want to come and have lunch with us? Then we're going to fish and swim."

"Thanks, I already ate and I just took out my stitches, so I better pass. Maybe another time."

Hannah wasn't sure she heard him right. "*You* took out your stitches?"

Birk chuckled. "Yeah. I can't believe I did it either."

"Didn't it hurt?"

"Not really. It just felt kinda weird. When I pulled the thread through my skin it felt just like thread pulling through my skin. Ha!"

"Ewww. No!" Hannah looked down at his leg, expecting to see a steady stream of blood, but there was none—just a couple of bandages. "Why didn't you go to the doctor?"

Birk shrugged his shoulders. "Dad's working long hours and hardly home. I didn't feel like walking that far. It was no big deal."

"Walk? You know, you could ask for a ride, Birk. My mom or dad would have taken you. Anyway, you don't have to eat and you don't have to get in the water. You can still join us to go fishing and we brought brownies for dessert. My mom is *the* best baker in town, in case you hadn't heard."

Birk smiled. "I think I did hear that." Then shrugged. "Thanks, Hannah. Maybe."

As Hannah walked away, Ransom barked and started to follow her. Hannah smiled as she bent down to give him a final pet. "See? Ransom wants to join us. I hope he can talk you into it."

~21~

A VISIT TO TURTLE LAKE

Birk wanted to follow Hannah to the lake, but her parents would be there. He wasn't sure he cared to see them. He also knew that wasn't really fair—it wasn't their fault his dad sold the land. *And they had to be nice people, right?* They rescued Hannah and her brothers and maybe even saved their lives. Hannah liked them. *Wasn't that enough?*

"I guess there's no reason for us to hold a grudge, Ransom. If it's too awkward, we'll come back. Will you behave if we go over there?"

Ransom barked and led the way through the trees.

When they reached the clearing by the lake, Hannah and her family were all seated on a blanket on the ground. Ransom ran ahead and announced their approach.

"Ransom!" Hannah shouted. "Hey, Birk! Mom, Dad, this is Birk McKenzie. He lives through those trees. Well, I mean, he's in my class and..."

Birk could tell Hannah was struggling with the introduction, but thankfully, Ransom chose that moment to jump on her and lick her cheek. "And this is Ransom, everyone!" Hannah said, laughing.

Hannah's dad stood up and reached his hand out for Birk to shake. "It's nice to meet you, Birk. I'm Robert. I hope you came hungry. There's plenty of food here."

"Yes, come and sit down, Birk." JoAnn added. "I'm JoAnn, by the way. It's so nice to meet you. How about a lemonade? Have you met Wes and Jamie?"

Birk looked from JoAnn, to Wes, then Jamie, but before he could speak, Jamie did.

"Hey, Birk! We've talked on the phone. You probably want to sit by Hannah, huh? Here, I'll move over." The smirk on his face suggested he might be trying to embarrass Hannah. Birk sat by Hannah, anyway.

He raised his hand in greeting. "Hi, everyone. I've already eaten lunch, but Hannah said something about brownies?"

JoAnn laughed. "Brownies! Yes!" She opened a bakery box and slid it across the blanket to Birk. "Help yourself. And here's your lemonade."

"Thank you," Birk said, happy to hide his face behind the drink.

"Hannah tells me you know a lot about trees, Birk," Robert said.

Birk shrugged and wiped the lemonade from his mouth. "I know a little, I guess. I grow Christmas trees with my dad and he's a woodworker so he taught me a lot. So did my grandpa."

"A woodworker, huh? Does he have his own shop?" Robert asked.

"No. I guess it's more of a hobby now, but he doesn't really have much time for it these days." Birk looked down at the brownie in his hand and started poking his finger into it. He was getting uncomfortable with Robert's questions. He felt like a bit of a liar at the moment. His dad *should* be a woodworker, but instead he's working in some factory doing who knows what.

"I noticed a tree over there with unusual bark and I'm not sure what it is. Maybe you know?" Robert asked.

Birk shielded his eyes and looked in the direction where Robert was pointing, just beyond the clearing near the lake.

"Does it have small berries?" Birk asked.

"Yes, it does," Robert said.

"Is the bark sorta warty looking?" Birk asked.

"Yes, that's exactly how I'd describe it," Robert said.

"It's probably a hackberry," Birk said. "Birds love the berries, but humans can eat them, too."

"Really?" Robert asked. "I didn't know that. I guess you do know your trees."

Birk smiled and took a bite of his brownie.

"Dad's going to build a cabin here!" Jamie said.

Birk stopped chewing. He looked at Robert. "A *log* cabin?" he asked.

"No," Robert answered. "I'm not interested in cutting down any live trees, Birk. I may clear away a dead or dying tree to use as firewood, but I've been storing reclaimed lumber from an old barn that I'd like to use for the cabin."

Birk nodded, then gave a relieved smile. "I always thought a cabin would be cool here."

"Has this area ever flooded, that you recall?" Robert asked.

"I've seen the water get as high as the bottom of the dock, so the sandy beach disappears, but I've never seen it higher than that," Birk said.

"That's good to know. We'll just set the cabin a bit away from the beach on that little knoll there," Robert said.

"Speaking of beach," Jamie said. "I'm getting hot. I'm ready to swim."

"Let's get the food wrapped up and put away and I'll join you," JoAnn said.

"I think I'll do some fishing," Wes said. "We have an extra pole if you want to fish, Birk."

"Thanks. I like to fish," Birk smiled.

Jamie stood with his hands on his hips, looking annoyed. "I suppose now you want to fish instead of swim. Huh, Hannah?"

Hannah ruffled Jamie's hair. "I suppose you're wrong, little brother." She ran for the lake, dropped her cover-up on the beach, and jumped in. Ransom and Jamie chased her to the water and jumped in after her.

~22~

ALL SMILES

Hannah couldn't wipe the smile off her face on the drive home. The view out the window was beautiful and the day by the lake was perfect.

"Geez, Hannah," Jamie said. "You've been smiling to yourself for miles. What are you smiling about?"

Hannah turned toward Jamie. "*You*, little brother! I'm just thinking how lucky I am to have you around *all the time*!" Hannah tickled him in the ribs to make him giggle.

"Yeah, I thought so," Jamie said. "Well, I like Birk, too, just so you know."

"Nobody said anything about Birk, did they?" Hannah said.

"I told you, I'm a detective. I can detect these things."

Wes smiled, shaking his head. "I like him, too, but somebody should let him know that when you borrow a fishing pole, it's not polite to catch the biggest fish."

~23~

A GOOD DAY GONE BAD

Birk smiled to himself as he walked back through the woods toward home. He stopped at the clearing to get the bucket and his backpack. Carrying that and the stringer full of fish was a little awkward; Ransom jumping at the fish was no help.

"Hey, back off, buddy. These are for Dad and me. You can have a nice big bowl of dog food when we get home."

The word 'home' was enough to set Ransom running off in that direction.

Though Birk only caught one fish, Robert insisted he take home all of them. He told Birk it would make a nice meal for two people, but not enough for their family of five. Birk knew his dad would appreciate fresh fish for dinner, and left-over cold fish was a favorite of theirs for breakfast.

Once in the kitchen, Birk dumped the fish in the sink and filled it with water. He gave Ransom a bowl of dog food and fresh water, then got busy cleaning the fish. He ran outside to the garden to bury the fish heads and guts. He knew it was good fertilizer, as long as the racoons didn't dig them up and eat them.

"I might as well dig up some potatoes while I'm here," Birk said.

Ransom barked from the front porch.

"Yes, I'm talking to myself," Birk called out. "Just eat your dinner!"

Birk dug up three fat potatoes to fry with the fish. He looked to the west and decided he had another hour before sunset. His dad should be home an hour after that. *That gives me time to finish my English paper.*

Birk took the potatoes inside, washed them and left them out to dry while he took a quick shower. He studied his stitch-removal job, pleased that the wound was staying closed. He patted it dry, applied a fresh pair of bandages, then sat down to work on his paper.

The books he checked out from the school library had proven useful in teaching him the history of certain Christmas tree varieties—like the Scotch pine—and how it made its way to America from its home in northern Europe. He updated his bibliography to include those books, then printed a copy of the paper that he could use to mark up for any corrections.

While Birk waited on the print-out, the phone rang. A glance at the caller ID confirmed that it was his dad's cell phone.

"Hi, Dad. Hey, didn't you tell me you aren't supposed to use your phone while you're driving?"

There was a long pause on the other end of the phone.

"Dad? I was just kidding."

"Birk, kiddo. I wish I was driving. Listen, I can't make it home tonight. I need to cover an extra shift and if I drive home, I'll get about two hours of sleep before heading back up here tomorrow. I called Boone and they are fine with you spending the night. Dillon is looking forward to it and they want you to go over for dinner, too. Boone will be there to pick you up in about ten minutes. Oh, I also arranged for him to take you to the doctor Monday to get your stitches out. I'm sorry I can't be there."

Birk couldn't hide his disappointment. He was looking forward to telling his dad about fishing with the Wheels and he was excited to be able to surprise his dad with a big fish dinner. "I don't need to," he said.

"Huh? 'Don't need to' what, Birk?"

"Any of it. I already have supper started and I don't need the stitches out."

"The doctor said the stitches should come out in seven to ten days, so Monday is it," Mick said.

"Yeah, but I already took them out."

Birk was startled by the anger in his dad's voice. "What do you mean you took them out?"

"It was no big deal. I looked it up on the internet and I used tweezers and scissors and it worked and nothing bad happened." Birk glanced down at his leg. "It's still fine."

"Birk, now that was just plain reckless of you! I didn't pay to have your leg stitched up just so you would do a foolhardy thing like that and risk getting it infected again. I really need you to show a little more responsibility when I'm not there."

Now Birk was angry. "Seriously? I *am* responsible. I don't need to go to Dillon's for dinner because I'm fixing *our* dinner—from the fish I caught on the lake and the vegetables I grew in the garden and that was after I mowed the lawn and worked on the trees. And I guess if you aren't coming home then you won't be helping me with the trees this weekend, either, will you? So, they'll just be my responsibility, too!"

Worse than his dad's angry voice, was his slow, quiet voice. "No. I won't. And you don't need to knock yourself out as far as the trees go. There isn't going to be a tree sale this year. Alright? It just isn't going to happen. I'm sorry. This isn't how I wanted the year to end for us, but that's the way it is. We can talk about it more when I get home, but I need to get back to work. Get your things ready to go to Dillon's. I'll see you tomorrow night."

"Wait! Dad! I didn't mean to get mad. I didn't mean to sass you. I can ask Dillon to help me with the trees. We can get it done."

"Birk, I decided about the tree sale before I called you. Your sassing me had nothing to do with that decision. There are just too many expenses involved and too many unknowns as far as my work schedule. I'm sorry, but there won't be a sale this year."

Birk's ears were ringing. His heart was pounding in his chest.

"Birk? Are you there?"

"Yeah. I'm here."

Birk heard his dad's frustrated exhale. "Birk, I need to get back to work. Would you please…"

"Right. You better go," Birk said.

"Birk! At least put Ransom in the house with you."

Birk hung up the phone in time to hear a horn honking from the drive. He rubbed his forehead and took a deep breath. He was in no mood for Dillon's chipper chatter. That much he knew. He hurried down the stairs and out the screen door as Dillon hopped out of the passenger side of his dad's truck. Ransom gave Birk a sympathetic whine and rubbed his head against Birk's leg.

"Hey, Birk!" Dillon greeted as he approached the porch. "Are you ready?"

"Hey, Dillon." Birk said, then waved to Boone. "Sorry you made the trip over here, but I just hung up from talking to Dad and didn't have time to call you. I'm not feeling all that great and I don't want you guys to catch whatever I have, so I'll stay here tonight."

Dillon took a step back. "Whoa, bummer. What is it? Do you think it's the flu? Christine Smiles threw up in class yesterday. Did you know that? It looked like grape nuts. The janitor shook some of that red sawdust all over the puke and then…"

"Dillon!" Boone yelled from the driver's seat. "Would you give it a rest?"

"Oh. Okay. Are you sure, Birk? Mom fixed meat-loaf."

"Sorry to miss it. You know I love meatloaf, but it would be bad if I threw up all over your dinner."

Dillon ran back to the truck and spoke to his dad as he opened the truck door. Boone leaned out the driver side window, "Sorry to hear you're feeling poorly, Birk. We're just a phone call away if you need anything, okay?"

"Thanks, Mr. Anderson." Birk waved as they pulled away, then held the door for Ransom. He shut it securely, walked up the stairs, and tore up his English paper.

~24~

THE CREEPS

Although Hannah was hopeful that they might find her bracelet, she was not looking forward to the trip back to Olga's house. It was hard for her to pretend otherwise.

"Hannah, you don't need to go back there at all," JoAnn said. "Robert and I can look for your bracelet—or anything else you might want from there. Would that be better?"

Hannah looked at Wes to see how he was feeling about going back. He shrugged his shoulders. "I don't mind looking for it, Hannah. To me, it's a future homeless shelter and that's what I'll tell myself while I'm there. Where all should I look?" he asked.

Hannah exhaled and smiled at her brother. "If you're okay with it, then so am I. You're right. It's going to be a homeless shelter and that's a good thing. Honestly, I've already looked nearly everywhere for it, except the desk. I couldn't get the desk open."

Jamie was studying a package of chocolate chips sitting out on the counter. "There's another place it might be."

"Where?" Hannah asked.

"What was her number one rule about what we weren't supposed to touch?" Jamie asked.

"Any of her snacks," Hannah said.

"Oh yeah. What was her number two rule?" Jamie asked.

"Her cat collection," Wes said.

"Right! I bet she hid the key under one of those cats," Jamie said, referring to the collection of ceramic cats that Olga treasured. "You know how she guarded those things like they were her precious babies!"

"Like you're doing with those chocolate chips?" Wes asked.

Jamie looked up and smiled. "Exactly."

"Okay, we'll look for the key under the cats," Robert said. "But I'll take a drill just in case we need to try the desk. Are we ready?"

"I'm staying here to help Momma Jo bake cookies," Jamie said.

Hannah ruffled his hair. "We know. Make sure you put the chips in the dough and don't forget to save a cookie for us, okay?"

"I will. One for you and one for Wes."

JoAnn rolled her eyes. "There will be plenty left

for you when you get home. Happy hunting, you two. I hope you come home with your bracelet, sweetie!"

The drive to Olga's house brought back a flood of bad feelings for Hannah, but not nearly as bad as when she stepped into the house. She really didn't care to touch any of the surfaces and when she brushed against the dining room table where Olga took her many meals, she cringed. *It's going to be a homeless shelter. It's going to be a homeless shelter. It's going to be a homeless shelter.*

"Why don't you wait in the car, Hannah?" Robert said. "Wes and I will be quick about this."

She brushed off her shirt where it had touched the table. "No, it's okay. It's going to be a homeless shelter, right?" But Hannah was no help with the search. She stood in the middle of the room and watched while Wes and Robert looked under each of the ceramic cats.

"These things are more creepy than cute," Robert said, picking up the largest cat with the hollow looking eyes.

Hannah shivered.

Robert picked up the final cat and set it down. "No key here," he said. "You guys move away from the desk so I don't cover you in sawdust." He turned on the drill and soon the lock fell to the floor. Hannah and Wes moved beside Robert as he pulled open the center drawer.

"Empty," they said in unison.

Robert pulled it all the way out and turned it upside down. He did that with each remaining drawer. When they were all out, he looked carefully inside the empty shell of a desk, ensuring nothing was taped inside.

"Nothing?" Hannah asked.

"Nothing, I'm afraid," Robert said. "I'm sorry, kiddo."

"That's weird. Why lock an empty desk?" Wes asked.

"I have no clue," Robert said. "Can you think of anywhere else she may have hidden it, Hannah? Somewhere in her bedroom, maybe?"

"No. I had to clean her room every week, so I've already checked every corner of the room and closet, every drawer and every pocket of every piece of clothing," Hannah said. "She must have taken it; or knowing her, she may have thrown it away."

"The medicine cabinet in the bathroom?" Robert asked.

"I checked there, too," Hannah said.

"What about the basement?" Robert asked.

"She never went down there, but I did laundry every week and I checked there just in case," Hannah said.

Robert nodded and gave Hannah's shoulder a quick squeeze. "If you're sure, then I don't want to keep you here any longer. Wes, do you want to look around in the garage for anything?"

"No, I'm good," Wes said. "Everything I wanted from there went with us to Horseshoe Hideout."

"Nothing from your bedroom?" Robert asked.

"The attic, you mean. No. We took all the good stuff," Wes said.

Robert glanced around the room. "In that case, let's go before Jamie eats his way through the cookie dough."

* * *

JoAnn and Jamie were sorry that they came back without the bracelet.

"You looked under each of the cats?" Jamie asked. "And the desk was empty?"

"Yes and yes. What was the point of locking an empty desk, anyway?" Hannah said.

"Who knows how her mind worked," Wes said.

"She would've locked her cabinets if she could. She just didn't want us in anything that was hers," Jamie said.

"Anyway, I can't think of where else it could be,"

Hannah said. "But I've been without it this long, so it's okay."

"Hmmm. There wasn't any artwork on the walls, so she didn't have a hidden safe to put her valables in," Jamie said.

"Val-u-ables, Jamie," JoAnn corrected.

"Val-u-ables, I mean. Her only val-u-ables were her snacks and her creepy cats."

"You're right about the creepy part—especially that one with the buggy eyes," Robert said.

"Oh," Jamie said. "You mean the one that lights up in the eyes?"

"Well, I didn't know it lit up," Robert said.

"I didn't know that," Hannah said.

"Yeah, there's a switch on the back."

"I missed that, completely," Robert said. "But, I don't think that would make it less creepy."

"No. It was creepy when it was lit, too," Jamie said. "Creepier. But the last few times I tried to turn it on, it didn't work."

"Jamie! You were always getting in trouble for touching those things. I can't believe you kept trying it," Wes chuckled.

"Well, she never bought us any toys! What did

she expect?" Jamie said.

"I'll let Denny know he can come and pick up the furniture. Do you want to see if Curtis wants those cats for the Wheel and Deal, JoAnn?"

"If it were up to me, I would say toss them, but I'll let Curtis decide since he's running the shop now," she said.

~25~

SAVED BY THE BELL

Dillon hadn't been as chatty with Birk on their daily rides to school and back. Birk wondered if it was because he'd heard about the tree sales and thought he better keep it to himself. Or maybe he just sensed Birk wasn't in the mood to listen.

But this Monday, Dillon had something important to say. He clutched his book bag in his lap and shifted nervously in his seat. "Hey, Birk?" he said. "I know your dad is working out of town and all, so I just wanted you to know that I can help you with the trees. I can come over after dinner on school nights or on weekends when I'm done with chores. Thanksgiving is less than a month away, so I know you have a lot to do to get ready for the sale. I could start helping you this week."

Birk glanced at Dillon with a half-hearted smile. "I guess Dad hasn't told yor dad everything, huh? We aren't selling trees this year, so I won't need help."

Dillon stared at Birk with his mouth half open. "But...why would he say that? You have a bunch of trees you could sell."

"Yeah, but that doesn't seem to matter. I guess it only mattered to Dad when Grandpa was alive. It isn't going to happen and I don't really want to talk about it, okay?"

Dillon looked down at his book bag in silence.

Birk nudged him gently. "Hey, Dillon? Thanks for the offer. I knew you'd help me if I needed you."

Dillon nodded, but silently fidgeted with his bag the remainder of the ride.

English papers had been turned in at the end of class on Friday. In the end, Birk re-printed the paper he had torn up and submitted it without giving it another look. He felt like a fraud turning it in, but he didn't really have time to pick another subject. Besides, Miss Barrett wouldn't have any way of knowing it was full of lies. He'd be lucky to get a C on it, considering he hadn't even proof-read it.

So he was shocked when Miss Barrett returned his paper with a bright red "A" at the top and "Read Aloud Please," underlined. He was very pleased, but also very shocked. *Well, he wasn't pleased about that read aloud part.*

He glanced across the aisle. Hannah looked up from her paper with a smile on her face. *Good. She must have aced hers, too.* Birk smiled back.

Miss Barrett finished returning the papers and then pulled the podium away from the wall. "Most of you did a fine job with your papers, and I have to say, I learned more than I thought possible about the Mississippi River, Black Hawk trails and the bats of Stars Cave. If you received a 'C' or below, I would like you to review the notes I've made and consider if you would like to rework your paper for extra credit. If you are interested, I will need the rewritten paper back by the end of the day tomorrow."

There was a collective groan in the room. "Tomorrow, really?" Nick Nadler asked.

"Quit your complaining, Nick, and please remove that hat. I am offering up one more day out of the goodness of my heart. Take it or leave it. Now, class, I thought you might enjoy hearing from a few of our writers on subjects that may not be familiar to you. I've selected three students to read their papers aloud and then we'll allow a brief question and answer session after each. Ava, would you please go first? Ava has written a paper on the origins of Perkins Park that I think you'll all enjoy."

Ava's paper was a hit. She shared that the popular Perkins Park of nearby Burlington was once a large cow pasture before it was sold to the wealthy Perkins family in the 1800s. In the winter, young children would sneak on the property to sled on the hills. In the fall, they would pretend to protect the apple orchard from foreign invaders.

When Mrs. Perkins discovered that her hired help had chased the young apple guardians off the property, she felt she needed to right the wrong. She had uniforms made for each of them with an invitation to return to guard the apples whenever they pleased. She also gave them each a bushel of apples to thank them for their service.

"So when you go sledding at Perkins Park," Ava said, "just think of all the kids throughout the years that have been doing that very same thing…even the Apple Tree Guard!"

"Thank you, Ava! Your paper was very well written and a delight. Any questions for Ava, class? No? Okay, Hannah, would you like to go next?" Miss Barrett asked.

Hannah read her paper about crinoids, the little sea creatures that lived before the dinosaurs and still live today. Her classmates were all ears as she explained how Iowa had once been under a shallow sea over 500 million years ago.

That sea eventually disappeared, but another covered the state more recently, around 200 million years ago. Deposits of fossilized crinoids were left behind. In nearby Burlington, the deposits were more than 200 feet deep and so varied (with over 300 species) that it is still considered the 'Crinoid Capital of the World'.

"One of Burlington's most important collectors of crinoids was Professor Wachsmuth," Hannah read. "He moved to Burlington from Germany and first stored his crinoids in a cigar box. It wasn't long before he had to move them to their own cabinet, then an entire room in his house. Eventually, he had so many crinoids that he put them in their very own fireproof house!

"Other scientists came to view his collection and considered it so important that he was convinced to move it all to Harvard University. So, when you see one of these fossils in the limestone walls and bluffs all around Flinthills and Burlington—maybe in your own backyard—remember that it used to be alive, living in a warm sea, hundreds of millions of years ago."

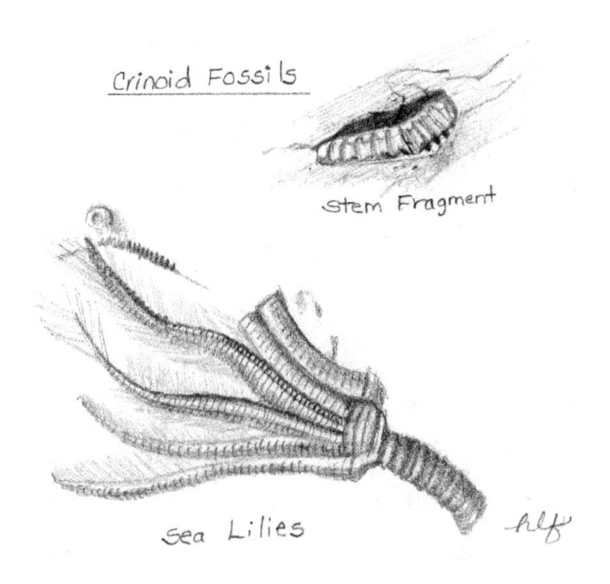

"Thank you, Hannah!" Miss Barrett said. "Are there any questions for Hannah? Yes, Nick?"

"So, Hannah," Nick began, scratching his head. "Are crinoids plants or animals or rocks?"

"Crinoids are sea animals," Hannah explained. "Certain varieties are called sea lilies, which sounds like they must be plants, but they're not. What we see today in Flinthills and Burlington are the fossilized remains."

Nick nodded. "Cool. I like your pictures, too. How do I get an original Hannah drawing of a crinoid?"

"Nick," Miss Barrett interrupted. "Maybe take that up with Hannah after class. Does anyone else have a question for Hannah? No? Okay, Birk, would you please read your paper for us?"

Birk wasn't sure about this. He wished he had spent more time proof-reading, but too late now. He cleared his throat and began. "The McKenzie Christmas Tree farm and forest all began when my great-great-grand-father moved here from Scotland over a hundred years ago."

Birk looked up occasionally to see if the class was listening or sleeping or watching the clock. He could always jump to the end if he was boring them. He was surprised to see all were awake and watching him with interest, so he read to the very end. He hoped he could deliver the final line without his voice cracking. He took a deep breath. "Hopefully, the McKenzie farm will live on to provide fresh cut trees for generations to come."

"Thank you, Birk!" Miss Barrett said. "You must be very proud of your family's tree farm. Oh my, we've got several hands in the air already. Let's start with Annie."

"Hey, Birk." Annie said. "I've always wondered which tree smells the most like Christmas?"

Birk smiled. "I guess that depends on what you're used to and what you like. The firs are probably the most popular scent—the balsam fir, Douglas fir and Fraser fir. But the balsams dry out kinda fast and the Douglas can't hold very heavy ornaments, so the Fraser Fir probably wins as most popular. My favorite is the Scotch or Scots Pine. It smells good, it doesn't dry out fast and the branches curve upward so they can hold heavier ornaments."

Miss Barrett called on several other students before calling on the last one. "Yes, Nick?"

"Aren't we supposed to be thinking about the environment and everything, Miss Barrett? So why is it okay to cut down a tree just to stick lights on it for a few days and then throw it away? I mean, we have an artificial tree. Isn't that what everyone should have?"

Miss Barrett looked hesitantly at Birk. "Do you have any thoughts on this, Birk?"

"Yes, I'll answer, Miss Barrett," Birk said. He figured somebody would ask this question—correction—he figured Nick would ask this question. "Our trees are planted and grown for the purpose of being harvested in six to ten years for Christmas. When we cut down a tree, we plant another tree, sometimes two. When Christmas is over and you're done with your tree, we don't want you to throw it away. We accept them back to turn into mulch, so they aren't wasted. Also, while our trees are growing, they are purifying the air around them. You can't say that about your artificial trees. In fact, the process of creating an artificial tree is probably bad for the environment, if you think about it."

Miss Barrett nodded and smiled at Birk. *She liked his answer.* But Nick wasn't done.

"Yeah, okay, but I've never heard of an artificial tree catching fire and burning down houses," Nick said.

Birk shifted his weight. "I don't know if they ever have or not, but it's no secret that you need to keep a fresh tree watered and make sure your lights are working and the electrical outlet isn't overloaded. You should turn the lights off at night or if you aren't going to be home. Oh, and you shouldn't smoke around your fresh tree, Nick. That's an important one for *you* to remember."

The class chuckled at that.

"Yeah, I don't smoke and my artificial tree doesn't need water, so what do you think about that?" Nick responded.

Birk just wanted to ignore Nick and take his seat, but there were two minutes left before the bell would ring. He was relieved to see Hannah's hand shoot up.

"Miss Barrett, can I ask a question before the bell rings?" Hannah asked.

"Please!" Miss Barrett answered.

Hannah stood up beside her desk and smiled at Birk. "So, Birk, how many trees do you usually cut down each year and how soon will you have to start cutting them to get them to the sale lot by Thanksgiving?"

Oh no. Birk looked down at his paper. *Should he tell the biggest lie right now*? He wished he could go back to Nick's question, because he didn't want to answer any part of Hannah's. He looked up at Hannah and saw her eager expression change to puzzlement. She was only trying to help, but she was making it worse. She slowly sat down.

Birk glanced up at the clock. He looked at Nick, and watched a slow grin spread across his face.

"Birk?" Miss Barrett asked. "Do you need the question repeated?"

Birk looked up at the clock. He didn't want to lie to Hannah, but she did say 'usually', so it wouldn't be a lie if he answered how many trees they *usually* cut even though this year it would be zero.

Birk cleared his throat. "*Usually*, we cut—"

'Rriinngggg!'

Finally! Birk now understood the expression 'saved by the bell.' He slowly stacked his papers as his classmates poured out of the room. He pulled the podium back to the wall for Miss Barrett, watching out of the corner of his eye for Hannah and Annie to leave. They waited briefly at the door, but moved on. He needed to explain himself, but he didn't trust his voice right now. He took his time gathering his backpack to ensure they were gone.

"Birk," Miss Barrett reached out and touched his arm as he tried to slip by. "You know Nick is just one boy—just one opinion. I loved your paper. The class loved your paper. We love the idea of your farm and many of us look forward to buying a tree from you each year."

"Nick doesn't bother me, Miss Barrett. I need to get to my next class." Birk kept moving toward the door.

"Sure. But, is everything okay?" she asked.

Should he lie? He didn't see the point. The whole town would know soon enough—at least those who were looking forward to buying a tree from them. He looked over his shoulder and tried to smile.

"Not everything."

~26~

SECRETS

After school, Hannah and Annie were outside waiting for Jamie.

"Was that weird in English class or what?" Hannah asked. "Did I imagine it?"

"Uh, no," Annie said. "That was definitely weird. You were just trying to help by getting Nick to stop asking his annoying questions. And Birk was doing so good. Why would he clam up at the easiest question of all?"

Jamie walked up with one of his classmates. "Hang on, Caleb," he said. "I need to get my notebook." Jamie set his backpack on the ground and reached inside to pull out the notebook Hannah had given him for his detective work. "Do you mean like this?" Jamie scribbled something and showed it to Caleb.

Caleb took the notebook from him and started writing in it. "No, like this," he said.

Hannah quit listening when she saw Birk exit the school. Annie elbowed Hannah in the ribs to make sure she had noticed.

"Ouch. I see. I see," she whispered.

Birk would have to walk past Hannah to get to his bus. Hannah didn't know if she should look away to avoid an awkward moment or act like nothing had happened. Jamie took the decision out of her hands.

"Hey, Birk! How's it going?" he asked.

Birk seemed fine when he answered. "Hey, Jamie. It's going okay. How's it going with you?"

"Good. Mostly good."

Birk smiled then looked up at Hannah and Annie. He let out a long sigh. "Hannah, thanks for trying to shut up Nick in English class. He can really get annoying sometimes, huh? Anyway, I need to explain something to you, I just, well, I mean, I didn't want to in front of the whole class, okay?" Birk glanced at his bus, then back at Hannah and Annie.

"What?" Annie asked. "Do you want me to leave? I'm not exactly the whole class."

"No," Birk said. "No. Don't leave. I just. I'll explain later, okay?"

Birk's discomfort was real. Hannah could tell he didn't really want to explain anything. He just wanted to run for the bus. "Later's fine, Birk. Don't worry about it."

Birk nodded and gave a half-hearted wave before running for the bus.

Annie elbowed Hannah in the ribs again.

"Umph, Annie! Why did you do that?"

"He does need to worry about it, Hannah," Annie said. "He needs to explain himself."

"Clearly, he didn't want to. Besides, he said he will. Just be patient, okay? And take it easy on my ribs!"

"Hold on a second, Caleb," Jamie said. "What does Birk need to explain, Hannah?"

"You don't miss much, do you?" Hannah said. "Nothing you need to concern yourself with."

"But maybe I can figure this out for you and then you don't have to wait," Jamie said. Hannah rolled her eyes, so Jamie tried another tactic. "What does he have to explain, Annie?"

Annie laughed and ruffled Jamie's hair. "You're a riot, Jamie, you know that? Hey, here's my mom. Is Wes riding with us today?"

"He has chess club, so it's just us," Hannah answered.

They piled into the car for the drive home.

Annie turned around from the front seat. "Hannah, have you thought about your Halloween costume yet?"

Before she could answer, Jamie jumped in. "Oh

yeah, you guys. My friend said the old library is open that night. They're giving out candy and they're going to have special exhibits, but most important of all, there's a chance we'll get to see a *real* ghost."

"Who told you this?" Hannah asked. "That boy you were talking to after school?"

"Caleb? No. Marla told me," Jamie said.

"Isn't the old library a museum now?" Annie's mom asked.

"Yeah, it is," Annie answered. "What's this about a ghost, Jamie?"

"Marla says her name is Miss Lilly. First she was a volunteer at the library—get this—over a hundred years ago! And then she became the first children's librarian in Iowa. She loved her job, but they made her retire before she was ready to quit. That's why she shows up there sometimes. I guess she wasn't done working. Anyway, Halloween would be the perfect night for her to appear."

"Well, at least she doesn't sound scary," Hannah said.

"I hope she's a little bit scary," Jamie said. "Can we go?"

"I'm okay with that plan," Annie said.

"I'm fine with that, too," Hannah said. "But we need to get Wes on board. Mom wants us to stay together wherever we go."

"Don't worry about Wes. He'll go," Jamie said.

Hannah and Annie chatted about the ads they had sold for the October edition of the paper.

"The flower shop wants me to paint a picture for their ad, so I'll work on that tonight and try to get it scanned and emailed, too. Mr. Galvin said he needs our ads turned in first thing in the morning. Will you have the bookstore ad done by then?" Hannah asked.

"Yes. I'll email mine tonight, too. He won't believe that we both got done early."

Annie's mom pulled the car up to the curb outside Horseshoe Hideout.

"Thank you for the ride, Mrs. Sterling!" Hannah said.

"Yeah, thanks Mrs. Sterling!" Jamie chimed in. "Bye, Annie!"

Annie popped her head out the window. "Hannah, call me if you hear from you-know-who."

Jamie closed the back door. "Birk, you mean," he said.

Hannah rolled her eyes and waved good-bye. She and Jamie went into the lobby. "Stairs or elevator?" she asked.

"Stairs. Hey, Hannah. I could help you get to the bottom of things with Birk if you would just answer a few questions."

"Jamie, I know you're a little genius and master sleuth and I know how badly you want a real mystery to solve, but believe me, this isn't it."

"You just won't tell me because it's about *Birk*," Jamie said. "But he's my friend too, you know."

Hannah had to smile at that. "I know. Hey, I heard you quizzing, who did you say? Caleb? What was that all about?"

"Oh. Changing the subject, huh? Real smooth, Hannah."

"Well?" Hannah prodded.

"You've got your secrets and I've got mine," Jamie answered.

~27~

OPTIONS

The days and nights of October marched on with Birk seeing very little of his dad. He came home every night, but very late. Birk delayed his bedtime just so he could spend a few minutes with him, knowing he would be gone in the early morning hours.

It was not a good time for them, but there was one big positive about the situation: it had eased Birk's anger about the land being sold and about the tree sale being canceled. He felt bad for his dad. Not only was he spending way too much time on the road, he was going to a job he didn't love.

He must have been really desperate to sell the land that had been in the family for so long. Knowing that the land now belonged to Hannah's family really hadn't changed Birk's life like he thought it would, but spending so little time with his dad was something he felt every day. He missed him very much.

He missed his companionship, his advice, and he missed his help with the trees. True, they wouldn't be selling any this year, but he still had to keep up with their care. The shearing—or shaping— had been done earlier in the year, but basal pruning still needed to be done.

Basal pruning involved cutting off the bottom twelve inches or so of branches. This needed to be done on the trees that were at least three feet tall. It was done to remove the energy-zapping foliage that would be removed anyway, once a tree was ready to be sold.

There were over fifty trees ready to be basal pruned so he had been working on it after school and weekends. He decided to try to finish another row before dinner. He needed that time to plan what he would say to Hannah about his earlier behavior, if he decided to say anything at all. He fed Ransom, freshened his water and then gathered his work gloves, pruning saw, and pruning shears from the barn.

He supposed the best thing to do would be to tell Hannah the truth. Then again, admitting to her that there would be no tree sale this year after she already knew about his dad selling off the land...well, he didn't want her feeling sorry for him.

He also felt like a fraud, really. Here he was telling his whole class how great it was to live on a Christmas tree farm that his ancestors started, when in reality, part of that farm was gone and they wouldn't even be selling trees this year.

Birk figured that was why he froze up when Hannah asked him about the tree sales, but he also didn't trust himself not to show his emotions. He felt strongly about his heritage and he had the sinking feeling it was all slipping away.

He didn't remember them ever skipping a year of Christmas tree sales. Maybe it was silly, but he felt he was letting down his Grandpa Mac. Like they were canceling a long-standing family tradition. For Birk, they were canceling his favorite part of the season.

He stood up and looked at the tree he had just trimmed. "Oops. I guess I need to focus."

Ransom was suddenly at Birk's side, looking up at him as though the conversation was intended for him.

"I was just talking to myself, boy." Birk scratched him behind the ears. "I know I got a little carried away on that one, but it'll be okay. We'll see what it looks like next year. I think that's enough for tonight."

Ransom barked in agreement.

Birk gathered up his tools and walked toward the barn. He still didn't know what he would say to Hannah. The whole truth and nothing but the truth, or nothing?

* * *

Birk was putting left-overs in the fridge when he heard a vehicle pull into the drive. Ransom stood up and wagged his tail. Clearly it was someone he knew. Birk looked out the kitchen door. *Dad's home?* He quickly pulled the left-overs back out of the fridge.

"Hey, Dad! I didn't know you'd be home so early. You want the rest of this soup?"

"Hi, Birk. Sure, that sounds good. I was hoping to get here before you ate, but sit down with me for a bit, okay?"

Normally, those words wouldn't bother Birk at all and he would welcome a chance to have a long talk with his dad. But lately any 'talk' was just his dad delivering bad news. Birk was feeling uneasy and the joy of seeing his dad home early was fading fast.

"Why are you home so early, Dad?"

Mick looked up at Birk, and back down at his bowl of soup. "How was school today?" he asked.

"School was fine. How was work?"

Mick pushed his soup bowl away from him and started rubbing his forehead.

"Dad?"

"Birk. I got permission to leave work early because I have to start pulling double shifts starting tomorrow. I need to pack my clothes and I need to tell you what your options are."

"Options?" Birk asked.

"Yes. Working double shifts will prevent me from coming home during the week—maybe even the weekends. You aren't going to stay here alone. To be clear, that is *not* one of your options. You've been on your own too much already. You either stay at Dillon's or you come with me and go to school in Dubuque."

Birk gripped the edge of the table. "What? School in Dubuque? No way."

"Like I said. It's an option. Although I'll miss you—more than I already do—I actually think it would be best if you stay at Dillon's. His folks are aware of the situation and you are more than welcome there and, frankly, if you decide to come to Dubuque with me, then it makes sense to rent or sell the farm. I won't be able to rent a place in Dubuque and keep this, too."

"Why does this sound like blackmail?" Birk said.

"It's not blackmail. It's the hard truth, son."

"If I don't stay with Dillon then you'll sell the farm?"

"That's not what I said. And maybe I said too much, but it sounds like they want me to do these double shifts through Christmas and that's too much time for you to be on your own. I can't have it. So, I need to know that you're staying with responsible adults while I'm gone, or you need to come with me."

"If I don't go with you, then I don't see you for two months?" Birk asked, anger now turned to concern.

"They have to give me a day or so every couple of weeks and I'll call when I can, of course, but that's about it. I'm really sorry that it's come to this, Birk. I haven't stopped looking for something closer to home—whenever I get a free moment—but this close to Christmas, it's not looking good."

Birk had a lump in his throat that he was having a hard time swallowing. Ransom crossed the room and rested his head on his lap. Birk stroked his neck until he trusted himself to speak.

"Okay. I'll sleep at Dillon's house."

"Look at me, Birk. Not just sleep. You'll go there after school and check in. You can ride your bike back over here to check on the house and feed the birds or get clothes you might need, but you will be back there in time for dinner and won't cause them any worry. And you will do your share of chores."

"Okay." Birk agreed. "Will they let Ransom come with me?"

"Yes. They said to bring Ransom. I'm sorry to put you through this. Believe me. It won't always be like this...one way or another."

Meaning what? It could get worse?

~28~

SECRETS REVEALED

When Wes returned from chess club that night, he was all smiles.

"You look happy!" JoAnn said. "Oh! Did you win your chess match?"

"I did!" Wes said, shrugging off his backpack. "I started out really strong and got control of the center board, but then my middle game was going nowhere. Dillon had two more pieces than me, but then I found a way to trap his queen and it was all over! Now, if I can just quit stumbling around in my middle game, maybe I could win some more."

"Oh, that's great, honey!" JoAnn said as she placed an aromatic casserole on the table.

"Way to go, Wes!" Hannah said, as she filled a wicker basket with freshly baked dinner rolls.

"If you have time after dinner, we can play a game or two," Robert said. "I might be able to help you with your middle game."

"Thanks, Dad. I have to read a chapter in Social Studies, but that shouldn't take long. I could definitely use the practice. I may have won this game thanks to the fact Dillon talks so much. Most guys don't like to talk during the game because they're trying to concentrate, but not Dillon. He goes on and on and on and the next thing you know, he's lost his queen!"

Soon, everyone was seated at the table and filling their plates.

"Doesn't Dillon live on a farm by Birk?" Jamie asked. "I know they ride the bus together."

Hannah glanced at Wes. He seemed a little uncomfortable as he answered.

"Uh, yeah. They're neighbors," Wes said.

"Thought so. Oh, before I forget, Wes, we're thinking of going trick-or-treating at the old library. Hannah and Annie are okay with that. Are you? Momma Jo wants us to stick together that night."

Wes scrunched up his face. "Why the old library? That's a museum now. Don't you want candy?"

"Yeah. They're giving out candy *and* they have a ghost!"

Wes' face brightened. "Oh. They're doing a haunted house thing?"

"No. I mean they have a *real* ghost." Jamie told them all the story of Miss Lilly.

"Real ghost. Right," Wes said, rolling his eyes. "But, I don't care. If that's what you guys want to do. We may need to hit some houses on the way there and back to make sure we get plenty of treats."

"Cool!" Jamie said. "I'll see if Caleb wants to go. Maybe you want to invite Dillon, Wes."

Wes shrugged his shoulders. "Sure." He noticed Jamie quickly look over at Hannah. "What?" Wes said. "Is there some reason I shouldn't? I know he talks a lot, but he's a good guy."

"It's fine with me," Hannah said. She glared across the table at Jamie.

"Is there some sort of secret language you three are sharing?" JoAnn asked.

"Yes, but what's *not* being said is the important part," Jamie said, trying to wink at Hannah.

Hannah rolled her eyes.

"Interesting," JoAnn said. "Well, Jamie, let me tell you in plain English that you need to quit stirring your dinner and actually eat it. You're helping me with the dishes tonight and then we have pumpkin bars to frost and decorate."

Jamie sat straighter in his chair and took a bite of dinner.

Hannah was glad to have Jamie distracted. She was sure the next thing out of his mouth would have been, 'and maybe Dillon would want to invite Birk.' Not that Hannah would mind if Birk was part of their Halloween group—in fact, that would be nice—but Jamie didn't need to be so weird about it.

After dinner, Hannah immersed herself in finishing the artwork for her school paper ad. The flower shop requested that she create a painting with a pumpkin and sunflowers to accompany their ad.

Hannah found that when her thoughts were troubled, she could *usually* lose herself in her drawing and painting. But tonight she was still thinking about Birk's reaction to her question in English class. *What had she said that made him clam up?*

Hannah was so distracted that she accidentally loaded her brush with violet paint instead of the burnt sienna (a reddish brown) she was going after. She swiped the brush across the pumpkin to give it shadow and was horrified...but then delighted.

"Wow! That looks really nice!" The violet wash gave the pumpkin an interesting and unexpected shadow. She liked it so much, she applied another coat and then tried a little in the shadows of the sunflower. "What a happy little mistake you are!"

"Uh. Are you talking to yourself, Hannah?" Jamie asked from her open doorway.

"Oh, actually, I'm talking to my painting." Hannah chuckled. "All done with the pumpkin bars?"

"Almost, but Annie's on the phone for you."

"Wow. I didn't even hear it ring."

Jamie shook his head as he walked back to the kitchen. Wes was in the living room setting up the chess board.

Hannah picked up the phone. "Hey, girl! I'm just finishing up the flower shop ad. What's up?"

Hannah should have guessed why Annie was calling. Of course she wanted to know if Birk had called to explain himself. "No, silly. I told you I'd call you if I heard from him." She turned around so her back was to her brothers. When she ended the call and turned to hang up the phone, Wes was leaning over the kitchen counter dipping his finger in the bowl of icing.

"Heard from who?" he asked.

"Really, Wes? That sounds like something Jamie would ask."

Wes shrugged. "Sorry. Just making conversation."

Jamie paused from licking icing from the spatula. "Heard from Birk, right?"

Hannah rolled her eyes. "Remind me to ask for a cell phone for Christmas. I think we're the only family in Flinthills that has a corded phone!" Hannah ignored the question and returned to her project. The painting finally dried enough to be scanned. She was all ready to hit the send button on the email when Jamie tapped lightly on her opened door.

"Yes?" she said.

Jamie plopped on her bed, sending her stuffed animals jumping. He bent down to pick up the chenille rabbit that had landed on the floor. It wasn't like him to be so quiet. Hannah stopped fiddling with her computer.

"What's up, Jamie?" she asked.

"I think I know why you and Annie have been whispering about Birk."

Hannah rolled her eyes. *Here we go again.* "What is it you *think* you know?" she asked.

"Well, Dillon played chess with Wes tonight, right? Wes said Dillon was jabbering during the match and told him that maybe he would be able to talk Birk into joining the chess club since he would be living with them—Dillon and his parents—while Birk's dad is working really long hours out of town. It's called double shifts."

"Wow. That would be tough. I'm sure Birk isn't happy about it, but I don't see what that has to do with how he reacted to my question."

"What question?" Jamie asked.

"See? You're just trying to get me to tell you what happened!" Hannah studied Jamie's face. At the moment, he really didn't look like an amateur detective on the prowl for a mystery to solve. He looked like Hannah's concerned little brother. She let out a long sigh, and told Jamie the full story.

"In that case, I think I know why he couldn't answer you," Jamie said. "Dillon said this wasn't the first bad news he got from his dad. First, he sold off part of the land, which we already knew, but it was Birk's favorite part of the land, according to Dillon."

"Yeah. He's probably right. He calls it the McKenzie Family Trees," Hannah said.

Jamie continued. "His dad also told him that they wouldn't be able to order any baby trees this year. They order baby trees every year to replace the ones they cut down at Christmas. But worse than that, he told Birk they aren't going to have a tree sale *at all* this year."

"What? Why would he say that? Their property is covered with trees to sell."

Hannah noticed Wes leaning inside her doorway. "Dillon's dad said it's because there are so many expenses in having a tree sale and also Birk's dad wouldn't be able to help with it because of his work," Wes said. "So he told Birk to forget it."

Hannah plopped down in her chair. "No wonder he didn't want to answer me. I thought I was helping him when I asked how soon they would start cutting down trees, but I only made it worse. And now he hardly sees his dad?"

"Yeah. And don't say anything," Wes continued, "but Birk's dad told Dillon's dad that if things didn't get better soon, he was going to have to think about renting out the the farm and moving Birk to Dubuque."

"Oh no!" Hannah said. "That would be awful! I wish there was something we could do to help."

"I know," Wes agreed.

"We have to think of something," Jamie added.

Robert came up behind Wes in the hallway. "Ready for that game, Wes? Hey, why does everyone look so troubled?"

"We're worried about Birk," Jamie blurted.

JoAnn popped her head behind Robert's. "What happened to Birk?"

Pretty soon, the entire family was in Hannah's room. The children took turns explaining the hardships that had fallen on Birk and his dad.

"I'm so sorry to hear that," JoAnn said.

"What does his dad do in Dubuque, do you know?" Robert asked.

"He works at a factory, but I'm not sure what kind," Wes said.

"Well, I admire that he's doing what he needs to do to provide for his family, but double shifts are hard, not to mention that drive." Robert said. "Hopefully, it's just for a short time and their life can get back to normal soon. Especially with the holidays coming up.

"And speaking of holidays and winter, I'd like to get the cabin closed in soon. The refinished lumber is ready, so I'm going to the lake Saturday with Denny to see what we can get done. Anyone want to join us?"

"I do!" the three said in unison.

"Oh, Jamie," JoAnn said. "Curtis is taking us to The Pumpkin Patch that morning, remember? I can take you out to the lake when we get back."

"Oh, yeah. I forgot. I'll be there after I pick out a pumpkin for us, guys," Jamie said.

Everyone started to leave Hannah's room, but Jamie stayed behind and slowly closed the door. "Since you told me your secret, I'll tell you mine," he said.

"Your secret?" Hannah asked. "Oh! The one you were discussing with Caleb?"

"Yeah," Jamie said. He plopped down on Hannah's bed. "I'm going to flunk first grade," he whispered.

"What?" Hannah said, then chuckled. "No you're not, Jamie! Why would you say that?"

"Because we have a really big project we're supposed to be working on and I'm not going to do it."

"You are *so* going to do it!" Hannah said. "What is it, anyway?"

"We're supposed to draw our family tree. We should have been working on it all last week, but I haven't. How am I supposed to do a family tree? I have two moms and two dads. I'm a freak."

Hannah walked over to the bed to sit beside Jamie. "Mrs. Penrose knows you're adopted and your friends know you're adopted. None of them think you're a freak. What did Caleb say to you?"

"He showed me how he was doing his, but he has one mom and one dad and two sets of grandmas and grandpas. He said it's okay if I put both my moms and dads on my tree, but how? I just want to do an easy one like Caleb's, but I don't want to hurt anyone's feelings and leave them off the tree, either."

"You should put them all on your tree. They are all your family," Hannah said.

"How do you fit all that on one tree?"

"Did Mrs. Penrose say they all have to be on one tree?" Hannah asked.

Jamie shrugged. "Not pacifically."

"Specifically," Hannah said. "What did she say, *specifically*?"

"She said how we show 'the tree' was up to us. It could be a diagram or an actual tree. She said we can use everyone's names or pictures or both."

Hannah squeezed Jamie's shoulders. "I think this sounds like fun, Jamie, and it sounds like she's leaving the design up to you. You know what might be fun?"

"Skipping the whole thing?" Jamie said.

"No, silly," Hannah said, giving Jamie a nudge. "What if you give everyone a different tree—their favorite tree?"

Jamie threw himself back against Hannah's stuffed animals and smacked his forehead. "Oh my gosh, Hannah. All that drawing? And how am I supposed to ask Mom and Dad their favorite tree? Or Grandma and Grandpa Russell? Or Grandma and Grandpa Faris?"

"Helloooo!" Hannah said, waving her hand in the air. "Your sister's an artist, remember? I can help you with Mom and Dad's favorite trees and we'll just guess for our grandparents. Whatdaya think?"

Jamie shook his head. "I'm not loving that idea."

Hannah's face suddenly brightened. "Wait!" She grabbed a tablet and pencil from her desk and quickly sketched. She showed the drawing to Jamie. "What about this idea?" she asked.

"Now, that I like! Thanks, Hannah. I think maybe I won't flunk after all!"

~29~

JAMIE'S BRIGHT IDEA

Birk had been staying at the Anderson's since Tuesday of the previous week. It felt pretty uncomfortable being in someone else's home, but Dillon's mom and dad tried to make him feel like he was part of the family. Birk helped with the dishes and farm chores so he wouldn't feel like a total burden and they were fine with him leaving on his bike to check on his own house and chores.

Sometimes Dillon went with him, but when he didn't, Birk always stole away to the clearing to feed the birds, watch the squirrels, and listen to the quiet.

On this particular Saturday, he decided to skip out on picking apples at Dillon's grandparents' farm so he could spend the day at his house. He didn't have anything special in mind, except to feed the birds and just chill on his own. As he entered his clearing—or rather the Wheel family clearing—he was pleased to find that Hannah's family still hadn't changed anything about it.

He filled the bird feeder while Ransom chased a rabbit, then he sat on the log to rest and think. He looked through the pines into the forest of maples, oaks and mulberries, now ablaze in their autumn glory. Iowa probably had one more week of spectacular fall colors before leaves turned brown and fell to the ground, or fell to the ground and then turned brown, in some cases. Birk loved this time of year. He felt like everyone respected trees in the fall, even if they took them for granted during the rest of the year.

He closed his eyes and listened to the rustle of leaves around him. The breeze was coaxing a sweet sound from the wind chimes. He heard a dove coo near-by and a 'tsk, tsk' from a squirrel. Birk opened one eye when he heard Ransom whimpering by his side. "Back from the rabbit chase?"

Ransom ignored Birk and stared down the path to the lake. He wagged his tail, all the while inching his way away from Birk and toward the path.

"Who's out there, boy?" Birk asked.

Ransom barked then looked back at Birk for permission to run.

"Come on, boy. Let's see what's left in the garden to go with the hotdogs I found in the fridge."

Ransom looked unsure.

"Didn't you hear me? I said *hotdogs*!"

At that, Ransom lost interest in the path, jumped on Birk and took off for the house. As Birk gathered up the bucket of bird feed he thought he heard voices. *Ah, that's what Ransom heard.* Birk was curious to see how far the Wheels had progressed on the cabin, but decided he better keep his promise to Ransom and fix those hotdogs.

There were a few ripe tomatoes and onions left in the garden. He picked the tomatoes and dug up the onions. He chopped up a little of each for his sandwich, but would take the rest to the Anderson's to share. Ransom got a dish of dog food along with his hotdog.

Birk cleaned up the dishes, then went through the house to water houseplants. When he finished, he went upstairs to pick out some lightweight sweaters for the next school week.

Dillon wanted him to go to the old library on Halloween, so he looked for something that could pass as a 'costume.' He had an oversized football jersey that his dad bought him at an Iowa Hawkeye game. That would work.

Birk shoved the clothing into a backpack he'd brought with him. He went outside and hung it on the handlebars of his bike. He still had a couple hours before Dillon and his parents would be home, so he decided to head back to the clearing. Maybe he could take a quick look at the cabin and say hi to Mr. Wheel.

* * *

Ransom didn't bother to wait for Birk, so by the time Birk pushed his way through to the lakefront property, Hannah was crouched on the ground petting him.

Mr. Wheel and another man were siding the cabin with reclaimed lumber. It looked great in the rustic setting.

"Hi, Birk!" Hannah called.

"Hi, Hannah. Sorry about Ransom barging in on you," Birk said.

Hannah laughed. "He can barge in any time!"

"Hey, Birk. Nice to see you again," Mr. Wheel said.

Birk waved. "Hi. The cabin looks great. I like the siding."

"That's the reclaimed lumber I was telling you about. I like it, too," Robert said.

Just then Wes popped his head out from inside the framed-in cabin. "Hi, Birk. Come inside and check it out. Is Dillon with you?"

Birk paused. "No. Just me and Ransom." *Why would he think Dillon should be with him? Has Dillon been telling his whole life story to anybody that'll listen?*

Wes looked uncomfortable. "Oh sure. I don't know why I thought Dillon would be with you."

"Maybe because Dillon doesn't know when to be quiet?" Birk said.

Wes chuckled nervously. "Yeah. I guess that's

fair. He's a talker. Sorry. It's none of my business. He just said you might start coming to chess club with him, since you're staying with him while your dad's out of town. Do you play chess?"

"Some, but not good enough to be in a club."

Wes shrugged his shoulders. "If you know the basic moves, you can be in the club. You don't have to be good." Then he smiled. "Besides, I need to be able to beat somebody."

Birk laughed, easing the tension of the moment.

Wes waved him forward. "Come on. Check out the inside."

The inside of the cabin looked bigger than the outside. Maybe that was because the lake view side was almost solid windows. Birk could see straight to the dock. Three fishing poles were in the water.

"Catch anything yet?" he asked.

"We have two on the stringer so far. This side of the cabin is going to be mostly windows with a door to the deck. Over there is the kitchen area. The bathroom is behind that wall. That thing over there that looks like a fireplace is going to be the fireplace." Wes smiled. "The stairs go up to a loft. Mom and Dad will sleep up there probably and we'll sleep down here.

"This is cool," Birk said. "I like that it's all open. Wow. Is that a skylight?"

Before Wes could answer, they heard a car pull up and a car door slam. "Oh, that's probably Mom and Jamie…"

They heard Jamie shouting. "Hannah! Hannah! I have the answer!"

Wes and Birk stepped outside to see what Jamie was so excited about.

Hannah laughed. "Calm down, Jamie! The answer for what?"

Jamie spotted Wes and Birk. "Oh, Birk! You're here. Good! I have the answer for your Christmas tree sales!"

"Oh no," Wes muttered. "Here we go."

"What?" Birk wasn't sure he was hearing Jamie right.

Hannah looked nervously at Birk then back to Jamie. "Jamie, wait."

"I know! I know! I'm calming down," Jamie said. He took two deep breaths then spilled his story. "Curtis took Momma Jo and me to The Pumpkin Patch this morning, right? But this isn't a place where you go pick out a couple of pumpkins from a pile." Jamie slowed down to make sure everyone was listening. "You. Cut.Them.Off.The.Vine.Yourself!" Jamie's eyebrows couldn't go any higher. "Get it?"

Hannah shook her head like she was trying to clear her thoughts. She glanced at Wes and Birk. "Jamie, what does that have to do with…Oh!" She spun around to look at Birk, her eyes huge. "Birk! What if you didn't have to cut the trees and haul them to town to sell? What if you let people come to your farm to cut the tree they want?"

"Yes!" Jamie said. "Exactly! It's the answer we've been searching for!"

Hannah swirled to look at Jamie. "Jamie! You're a genius!" She reached for him, but Jamie was too fast.

"Please, don't start kissing me, Hannah."

Birk felt all eyes on him. He was too shocked and embarrassed to share the excitement. "You've been searching for an answer? But I never told you there wouldn't be a sale this year, so how?" Birk's face suddenly relaxed, the confusion gone. He could feel his ears start to burn. "Dillon, right?"

Mr. Wheel put down his hammer and walked toward Birk. "What Jamie's suggesting is worth looking into, Birk. You have the perfect set-up for folks to come to you. I would think that would eliminate a lot of the expenses of selling trees in town."

Birk's head was spinning. He knew Mr. Wheel was talking to him, but he wasn't taking it all in. His head was trying to figure out how he felt about Jamie's suggestion, Dillon's betrayal, and how he could quickly vanish from this scene. Birk had never worked up the courage to tell Hannah why he behaved the way he did during English class, but it seems he hadn't needed to. *Telephone, telegraph, tell a Dillon.*

"You may wish Dillon had kept quiet," Mr. Wheel continued, "but I'm sure he had good intentions. He shared your situation with Wes because he cares about you. Give this some thought, Birk, and talk it over with your dad. We'll help in any way we can. If you think I might be able to help convince him, I'll be happy to talk to him."

Mrs. Wheel reached out and touched Birk's shoulder. "Birk, we would love to come to your farm to buy our Christmas tree. I could see it being a highlight of the season. And I'm sure we're not alone."

Birk tried to smile, but wasn't sure he pulled it off. "I'll think about it, thanks. I better go now. Come on, Ransom." Ransom looked back at the Wheels, but turned and followed Birk through the trees.

Birk couldn't get out of there fast enough. As soon as he was out of sight, he ran for the clearing and kept going. He didn't stop until he reached the front porch. He plopped onto the porch swing and covered his face with his hands.

How could Dillon go blab to everybody about his personal stuff? Why did Dillon's dad have to tell Dillon everything anyway? Doesn't he know what a big mouth Dillon is? I'm never going back to that house. He's a traitor!

Birk felt Ransom rest his head on his knee. He dropped his hands from his face, bent down and hugged him. "You know you're my best friend, right? But I really, really miss Dad. I wish he was here."

Ransom whimpered.

Birk sat up and finally allowed himself to really think about Jamie's idea. He liked it. *Why had they never considered having people come to the farm to cut their own tree? Knowing Grandpa he probably thought 'city folks' wouldn't want to come to a farm. What would the expenses be anyway?*

No parking lot to rent. No men or high school boys to hire to cut, wrap and haul the trees. No truck rental. No chance of cutting more trees than can be sold, so no waste. They may still need to wrap the trees, though.

Is Dad so set against a tree sale that he wouldn't consider this option? "There's only one way to find out, Ransom. Let's go inside and call Dad."

Birk was nervous about sharing the idea with his dad, but gained courage when his dad let him talk without interruption. At one point he even replied with a 'hmmm'. Birk continued with more confidence as he explained the breakdown of expenses.

"We wouldn't have to rent a wrapper, son. Just buy some twine so they can tie the tree to their car roof. If they have a pick-up truck, they won't even need twine."

Birk could hardly contain his excitement. *Not only was Dad not saying 'no', he was offering ways to make this work!*

"The biggest drawback I see to this, is me not being there to help. But let me give this some thought and I'll give Mr. Wheel a call. Head on over to Dillon's and I'll call you there."

"Thanks, Dad," Birk said.

So, I guess I'm going back to the traitor's house. Birk wondered if he would end up thanking Dillon for being such a blabber mouth. He sure hoped so.

~30~

IT'S A GO!

Hannah couldn't wait to call Annie when she got home. "We have to convince him," she said, cradling the phone with her shoulder while she wrote in her notebook. "But, Annie, you can't say *anything* to *anyone* about this. Birk was really upset that we knew the tree sale had been canceled. He wasn't happy that we heard about it from Dillon. Anyway, I hope he talks to his dad soon. I'll keep you posted! Bye!"

As Hannah turned to hang up the phone, Jamie stuck a piece of paper in her face.

Hannah jumped. "Geez, Jamie! You startled me! What's this?"

"While you were on the phone, we've been making a list of things that we think Birk will need for the tree sale."

Hannah smiled. "Aren't you so helpful! Let's see, saws, twine, sleds or wagons, hot chocolate and cookies. Hmmm. Let me guess who came up with that idea?"

Jamie smiled. "Don't you agree they would make Christmas tree cutting even more fun? Oh. Add marshmallows, too, okay?"

Just then, the phone rang. "Probably Annie," Hannah said. She glanced at the caller ID. "Nope. Not her number." She picked up the phone. "Hello? Yes, he is. Just a minute, please." Hannah set the phone down. "Jamie, tell Dad he has a call."

Jamie ran to get his dad, then followed Hannah into her room to chat about his school project. "Hannah, I've been thinking about the family tree project and I was wondering if you could make them apple trees? That way I can draw an apple for every name."

"Sure. I was just about to get started on that." Hannah said.

Just then Wes appeared at Hannah's door. "What are you guys working on?"

"My family tree stuff," Jamie said.

"I don't think I've ever heard so much talk about trees as I have in the past couple of weeks. Birk's trees, family trees, Christmas trees," Wes said.

"I know, right?" Hannah said. "But where would we be without them? The family kind and the other kind, too?"

During the pause in conversation, the children heard Robert finishing his call in the kitchen. "I'll let you know if we run into any issues, Mick, but I think this is going to work out fine. I appreciate you giving this a chance—my family's looking forward to helping Birk make it a success. We'll talk soon. Bye."

Hannah gasped and looked at her brothers with wide eyes. "He said yes!"

Robert appeared at Hannah's door, grinning. "That was Birk's dad. The tree sale is on! He's going to be able to come home for Thanksgiving and can help the day of the sale, but asked if we could help Birk get everything set up ahead of time."

JoAnn peaked over Robert's shoulder. "Oh! That makes me so happy! Has he told Birk yet?"

"He was going to call him right after we ended our call. Maybe give him thirty minutes or so, then one of you can call Birk and see how he's doing. Maybe make plans to get things organized."

Wes and Jamie both looked at Hannah. "Yes, I'll call him," she said.

Robert continued. "His dad has given me a few items to consider here, which shouldn't be a problem. His main concern is traffic and parking, if there's a good turn-out. Why don't you mention it to Birk and see if he wants us to drive over and check the property."

"I will." She looked at her bedside clock. "In twenty-five minutes," she added, smiling.

"This is awesome!" Jamie exclaimed, clapping his hands.

Wes picked him up and spun him around the

room. "My genius little brother!"

Everybody laughed.

"Can I call Curtis and tell him?" Jamie asked. "I told him about Birk's trees and if he hadn't taken us to the pumpkin patch, I wouldn't have thought of the cut-your-own plan…maybe. But, can I call him?"

JoAnn laughed. "Yes, you may call him, but keep it short so Hannah can call Birk."

"I need to call Annie, too, but I'll call her after I talk to Birk."

"Okay. Wes, you want to help me with the popcorn? Family movie starts in an hour," JoAnn said.

In the meantime, Hannah turned on her computer to research the shape of an apple tree.

~31~

HALLOWEEN

A smallish Iowa Hawkeye and an even smaller scarecrow sat in the backseat of Boone Andersons's truck. "Do you boys know what time you'll be done tonight?"

"We're going to Hannah and Wes' after the library and Mr. Wheel is bringing us home, Dad," Dillon answered.

"Oh. Your Mom said something about that. You're having a planning meeting for the Christmas tree sales, right?"

"Yep," Dillon said.

Boone glanced in the rearview mirror. "Be sure to include me and your Mom in the plans, Dillon. We're going to have my folks over for a couple days, but you can help Birk the day after Thanksgiving and we'll be available that Saturday." Boone said.

"Okay, Dad," Dillon said.

"Thanks, Mr. Anderson," Birk said.

"Birk, you've been staying with us for a while now. Would you please call me Boone?"

Birk smiled. "Okay. I will." He glanced over at

Dillon, decked out in bib overalls and straw hat. Straw was sticking out from his hat, neck, bibs and sleeves. "Doesn't that itch?" he asked.

"You better believe it," Dillon answered. "I should have gone with the cowboy idea."

Birk rolled down his window as they left the gravel road of the country and entered the paved streets of Flinthills. The air was crisp and fresh, with just a hint of woodsmoke coming from nearby chimneys. The reds of the sugar maples and yellows of the gingko trees stood bright against the fading blue sky. A cool breeze picked up a cascade of falling leaves and twirled them into a colorful dance above the pavement. It was a perfect night to be out with friends.

"Well, here's the old library. Are those your friends?"

"Yep," Dillon said. "That's Wes dressed up as Huck Finn, for sure. Thanks, Dad!"

"Yes, thanks, Mr., er, Boone!" Birk said, smiling.

"Have a good time, boys. Oh, wait. One of you forgot your flashlight there on the seat."

"Oops, that's mine," Birk said. He grabbed the flashlight and slammed the door, waving to Boone as he pulled away.

Birk couldn't help but laugh at the cast of characters lined up on the sidewalk in front of him.

"Hey, Huck!" Dillon said. "We're almost the same!"

"Aren't you a scarecrow?" Wes asked.

"Yeah, but if you take away the straw, we're close," Dillon said.

"Well, I think my costume would be better without shoes, but Mom said no way," Wes said.

"Don't worry. You look like Huck," Birk said. "The suspenders are great. Nice witch costume, Annie."

"Thanks, Birk! My friend, Roberta, made it in like two hours. Can you believe it? I swear, nobody can sew as fast as that girl."

"You look like a real artist, Hannah," Birk said. Hannah was wearing a French beret, a painters smock smeared with paint, and even had paint smeared on her cheeks.

"She *is* a real artist," Annie added. "You should see her drawings."

"Oh yeah," Birk said. "I remember the pictures you drew of the crinoids. Those were good."

"Thanks," Hannah said.

"Who's this Sherlock Holmes guy with you?" Birk asked, smiling.

"It's me, Birk! Can't you tell?" Jamie said.

"Oh yeah!" Birk said. "Hi, Jamie. Is Albert Einstein your friend?"

"Yeah. This is my friend, Caleb, you guys. He's as smart as Albert, too."

After introductions were made and costumes critiqued, the group entered the museum. The historic old building was decorated for the occasion with exaggerated spider webs and oversized plastic spiders. A huge jack-o-lantern sat on top of the receptionist's desk. A table full of treats stood in the rotunda area. A large, black caldron sat in the middle of the table.

Miss Linda, the museum receptionist, stood by the treat table to greet them. "Help yourselves to punch and cookies, everyone! You can also take a sack of candy there beside the cookies before you leave. Feel free to look around at all the displays, but the section over here to my left may be of special interest to you since it is a display of the so-called haunted buildings around town."

"Sweet!" Dillon said.

Jamie raised his hand. "Excuse me, Miss Linda. Where does Miss Lilly hang out?"

"Miss Lilly?" Linda looked puzzled, but then chuckled. "Oh! Miss Ann Elizabeth Lilly! You've heard about her, have you? Follow me and I'll show you her picture."

Jamie and his group followed Miss Linda to the narrow hall on the other side of the rotunda. It included many photos of the museum when it was a real, working library. The largest photograph was of a very proper looking Miss Lilly. She was dressed in a long skirt with a high-necked, ruffled blouse. Her hair was pulled into a loose bun at the nape of her neck.

"This photo was taken roughly a hundred years ago from the old reading room across the way," Miss Linda explained. "You'll notice that no matter where you stand, it's as if Miss Lilly is staring right at you."

Jamie tried several different locations. "Yep. She's looking right at me."

"She liked to keep her eye on everyone to make sure they were behaving," Miss Linda said, smiling. "But she loved it here and never wanted to leave."

"And maybe hasn't actually left?" Jamie suggested.

"Have you ever seen her walking around at night?" Annie asked.

"No, not me, but…" Miss Linda didn't finish her sentence.

"But what?" Jamie asked.

"But…I always close up before dark." Clearly, Miss Linda was done talking about ghosts. "Now, if any of you need a restroom, there is one right over here." Miss Linda pointed out the 'His/Her Restroom' behind her. "Oh, yes. Somebody asked me about the arrow-head collection. It's in the room across the way where the haunted house display is located, right next to the crinoid display cases.

"Over here guys!" Jamie said. "Let's check out the haunted houses."

"Yeah," said Hannah. "I want to see the arrow-heads and crinoids, too."

"You guys go ahead," Dillon said. "I need to use the restroom. I'll be right back."

Birk was sure he wouldn't be right back, not with all the undressing he would have to do. "Be careful not to lose all your straw," he warned.

The rest of them followed Hannah and Jamie across the rotunda to the other side of the museum. They quickly looked over the arrowheads and crinoids, but took their time in front of the pictures of the so-called haunted structures around town.

"Wes," Hannah said, "why don't you read the stories to us so we aren't all crowding around getting into each other's way."

"Sure. I'll start here with this old house on Main Street. Can everyone see the picture? Creepy, huh? This is what it says." Wes began reading.

"'There is a legend about this old house that goes back more than one hundred years. The legend surrounds the old grandfather clock believed to be the hiding place for the remains of …' "

Suddenly, the entire museum went totally dark!

Gasps and screams filled the darkness.

Birk heard a ripping sound nearby. "Let go of my costume!" Annie cried.

"What?" Hannah cried. "Are you okay, Annie?"

As Birk's eyes adjusted to the dark, he noticed the lights on the photo gallery across the hall had not gone out. They weren't doing much to help their current situation, though. He fumbled with his flashlight and turned on the switch. "It's just caught on something,

Annie. Hold still. There, you're loose now, but there's a hole in it now."

"Oh, brother" she said. "I've had it on for one measly hour."

Miss Linda addressed the crowd. "Please remain calm everyone! Did someone flip the light switch? Would whoever turned off the light, please turn it back on?" When nobody answered, she continued, "Well, hold on. I've got a flashlight in my desk. Let me see now. Where's my desk…"

Birk heard someone running toward them. He flashed his light in that direction. *Dillon!* He forgot about him being in the restroom. Dillon was trying to buckle his bib overalls while he ran towards Birk. Straw flew off his costume in all directions. His hat flew off behind him. That's when Birk saw an image he couldn't believe.

"What's *that*?" he whispered. An eerie image appeared from the direction of the bathroom and seemed to be floating straight toward them.

"It's her!" Jamie said. "It's Miss Lilly! She's coming this way!"

Annie screamed. "A ghost!" Then rrriiippp! "Oh my gosh! This costume!"

Birk was frozen in place. He couldn't believe what he was seeing. It was definitely Miss Lilly and she was definitely moving toward them…until, suddenly, she was gone.

He turned the light back toward the group. Dillon no longer looked like a scarecrow…just scared. Hannah had her hand over her mouth, eyes about to pop out of her head. Wes' mouth gaped open in disbelief. Caleb's wig had turned sideways and his mustache was now stuck to his lab coat. They all looked like they had just seen...well...a ghost!

Except for Jamie. He looked more excited than scared. "Wait 'til Marla hears about this!" he said.

"Why can't they find the light switch?" Annie said. "Let's get out of here! It's too creepy!"

"Wait!" Jamie said, and started toward the re-stroom, just as Miss Linda found the light switch.

"Jamie, what are you doing?" Hannah called to him, then slowly followed.

"Did you notice how Miss Lilly looked just like her photograph?" Jamie asked.

He's right. Birk thought. They all followed Jamie across the hall. Annie trailed behind, clutching her torn costume.

The restroom door had slowly swung shut after Dillon's hasty escape. Jamie opened the door a crack, peaked in, then turned towards his friends with a big grin on his face. "Just as I thought! There's a mirror on the door. Look!"

Jamie pulled the door open wide until the full-length mirror reflected the full-length photograph of Miss Lilly hanging a short ways away. As Jamie moved the door, Miss Lilly appeared to be moving.

"Oh!" Annie said, then started laughing. Soon they were all laughing, relieved that there was a logical explanation for what they had seen.

Miss Linda also watched Jamie's demonstration. "Well, I'll be," she said. "I never realized that before."

"Do you guys want to finish the haunted house display?" Wes asked.

"No!" Annie insisted. "I don't want to know what is hanging out in that grandfather clock you were reading about!"

"I'm okay if we do some trick-or-treating and head for our house," Hannah said. "Are you guys okay if we leave?"

Everyone looked around at each other and nodded.

Jamie picked up Dillon's hat and handed it to him.

"Maybe we should sweep up this straw before we go," Birk said.

"Sorry, about that," Dillon said. "It was creepy in the dark restroom."

"Don't worry about the straw," Miss Linda said. "I'll get a broom and sweep it up. It wasn't your fault the lights went out. Now don't forget to grab a bag of candy when you go." She bent down and whispered something to Jamie that made him smile.

As they grabbed their candy to leave, Jamie took two.

"Jamie?" Hannah asked. "What are you doing?"

"Shhhh," Jamie responded. "Miss Linda told me to take two. She said I've given her an idea for a new Halloween attraction for next year."

~32~

THE PLANNING COMMITTEE

As soon as they got outside the museum they all started to talk at once.

"Oh my gosh! That was so cool!" Dillon said. "At first we thought it was a ghost and then it wasn't a ghost. But I don't know. Maybe it was a ghost and *she* turned off the lights!"

"Yeah, who turned off the lights, anyway?" Annie asked.

"It was probably just a prankster," Wes said.

"Maybe Nick Nadler was there," Birk said.

Hannah wasn't sure if Birk was kidding or serious, but she tried to think if she had seen Nick. "I don't remember seeing him, but it would be just like him to try to scare everyone." She put her arm around Jamie's shoulder. "But you weren't scared, were you?"

"No. It was fun. For a few seconds there was an actual mystery!" Jamie said.

"And you solved it!" Birk said.

"Seriously, dude!" Annie said. "I was freaking out and you just walk on over in your little Sherlock Holmes costume and just like that! Mystery solved!"

Everybody laughed. Jamie tipped his Sherlock hat and took a bow. "Come on guys," he said. "Momma Jo has pumpkin bars and hot chocolate for us."

"I told Mom I would help her give out candy after the museum, so I should probably head home," Caleb said. "I'm this way."

"We'll walk you home, Caleb," Wes said. "We can trick-or-treat at the houses between here and your house."

They stopped at every house between the museum and Caleb's, trying their best to fill their bags with candy.

"Wait a sec, you guys. I'll give you some candy before you go," Caleb said. He ran inside and returned with a large candy dish. "Take two, everyone!"

As Jamie reached for his, he whispered to Caleb, "I haven't told Hannah yet, but I got an 'A' on my family tree poster! Cool, huh?"

"That's great, Jamie! You aren't going to flunk now!" Caleb said, with a big grin on his face.

"I know! So maybe we can be in second grade together next year. See ya tomorrow, Caleb!"

They all said their good-byes, then continued to hit the remaining houses before arriving at Horseshoe Hideout.

"Wow. An elevator!" Dillon said, as he entered the lobby.

"Shall we ride or walk?" Hannah asked.

"Ride!" Dillon answered for the group.

"Yeah, we've been walking all night," Jamie said.

So the witch, the artist, the football player, Huck Finn, and Sherlock Holmes all boarded the elevator to the third floor.

"Come on in everyone," Hannah said. She introduced her parents to Dillon, then led the group to the kitchen. She poured hot chocolate for everyone while JoAnn set out the pumpkin bars.

"Did you have any trick-or-treaters in the lobby this year, Mom?" Hannah asked.

"We had quite a few, actually, until right around eight o'clock. Did you have a nice time at the museum?"

"Don't answer, you guys!" Jamie said. "I'm going to tell Momma Jo and Poppa Bob all about Miss Lilly!"

JoAnn chuckled. "Bring your treat out to the living room and tell us all about it, Jamie."

Hannah and her group settled at the kitchen table. "I'll be right back," Hannah said. "I need to grab my notebook and I'll get you a safety pin for your costume, Annie. It almost lasted one night!"

Annie laughed. "You mean one hour, but don't tell Roberta. I don't want to hurt her feelings. Anyway, it was Miss Lilly's fault."

"Or whoever turned off the lights," Wes said.

"Which could have been Miss Lilly," Dillon said.

Hannah fetched the safety pin and her notebook containing the list of 'To-Dos' for the Christmas tree sale. "When our dads talked, Birk, your dad was a little concerned about parking," Hannah said.

"Yeah, we talked about that," Birk said. "We decided to put up a couple of saw-horses in the grass by the drive. We'll stretch a rope between them and hang a 'Park Here' sign from the rope. That way the drive will be clear for backing up and leaving."

"Good! Parking solved. A question we were wondering about, is if you have to tag each tree with a price?" Hannah asked.

"No," Birk answered. "The customer cuts down the tree and when they bring it to me to make their payment, we'll use our measuring pole to give them the final price. We decided to keep last year's price of ten dollars a foot."

"Do you have a sign you can hang that gives them pricing info?" Annie asked.

"We have a sign, but I'll make a new one since the set-up is different," Birk said. "Like, I want to tell them to cut the tree to the ground. We don't want a bunch of twelve inch stumps all over the property."

"Oh yeah. That would be bad," Dillon said.

"We can use the porch for the check-out stand," Birk said. "We'll have the saws there and I'll have the sign by the saws so everyone will see it. Speaking of saws. I checked the barn and we have four."

"We have two," Hannah said.

"My dad has two we can use," Dillon said.

Just then Jamie popped into the kitchen.

"Will the hot chocolate be at the check-out stand, Birk?"

"Hot chocolate?" Birk looked worried. "I hadn't thought about that."

"Oh, don't worry," Hannah said. "We'll bring the hot chocolate and some Christmas cookies. We have a folding table we can set up wherever you think best."

"Oh, cool," Birk said. "There are side steps onto the porch so you could have the hot chocolate on the side and I'll have the check-out stand at the front steps."

Annie cleared her throat and waved her hand. "So, Birk," she said. "We got the okay from Mr. Galvin to print your English paper in the school paper. It comes out the second week of November. We're also going to put an ad for the sale in the same paper, right next to the story—with your permission, of course."

Birk scrunched his nose. "Do you think it's good enough to go in the paper?"

"What?" Annie said. "You got an A! And we all loved it!"

Birk shrugged. "Okay. If you think it will help," Birk said. "How much is the ad?"

"It's twenty-five dollars for a half page, but Mom and Dad said they'll cover it and you can pay them back after the sale."

"I just have to sell one short tree to pay you back, so let's do it." Birk said. "And thanks, you guys. You're really nice to be so excited about helping and coming up with all these good ideas."

"Are you kidding?" Annie said. "This is going to be fun! And we haven't even talked about the posters we're going to hang around town!"

"Wow. That's great," Birk said. "I hope someday I can pay you back for all your help."

"It's nothing," Hannah said. "Besides, we've been wanting to traipse through your farm since the first time we drove by. It'll be fun! Oh, that reminds me. I think we should have a sign posted at the end of Mason Road to direct traffic toward your house. Otherwise, people might get lost. Maybe one at your drive, too."

"Good idea," Birk said. "The Johnsons live at the end of Mason Road, so I'll call them and get permission to put a sign in their yard. We have one we can post at our drive, so I just need to make one new one. We have lumber in the barn that we can use."

"Perfect!" Hannah said. "Do you have paint, too, or do you want me to help?"

"I have paint, but you're the artist, so I could use your help," Birk said.

"Happy to!" Hannah said. The group briefly discussed a few more items, then Hannah read through the complete list of tasks they had identified. "Did I miss anything?"

"I think that's it," Birk said. "I'll see if Dad can think of anything else. He'll definitely be home on Thanksgiving and the day after, so he can help us, too."

Hannah smiled. "I'm glad," she said. "That he'll be home, I mean."

Birk smiled. "Yeah, me too."

* * *

After Robert and Hannah returned from taking everyone home, Jamie padded out into the living room in his pajamas, dragging a rolled up poster behind him.

"Okay, everyone! I know it's my bedtime, but I didn't get a chance to show you my finished family tree. We got them back today with our grades and since you're all on here, I thought I would show you that…".

Jamie unrolled his poster board and held it wide open for his family to see. "Ta da! I got an A! And this is what she wrote on the back. Wait a sec. Hannah, what's this word."

Hannah whispered in Jamie's ear.

"Okay, it says 'Jamie, this may be the most *unique* family tree I have ever seen! Well done!' "

Everybody oohed and aahed as Jamie smiled proudly. "And I just want to say that I couldn't have done it without Hannah."

"Oh, that's so sweet!" JoAnn said. "Look at those two trees, how they form a heart right in the middle! And everyone has their own apple. I just love it, Jamie!"

"Using two trees was Hannah's idea," Jamie said.

"But Jamie painted it and labeled it himself," Hannah said. "And it was his idea to make them both apple trees, so everyone would be an apple and…"

Suddenly, Hannah noticed something on the poster that hadn't been there before. "Oh, what did you add down there at the bottom of the Russell-Faris tree, Jamie?" She squinted but couldn't make it out.

"Oh, yeah." Jamie said. "It's just a little rotten apple that fell off the tree. I didn't want to leave her off completely. See. Right here it says 'Aunt Olga'."

Hannah sat back on the sofa, covered her mouth, and tried not to laugh.

JoAnn tried not to laugh, but accidentally snorted.

Wes and Robert didn't bother to hold back. Soon, they were all laughing—Jamie the loudest of all.

~33~

THANKSGIVING

Birk was thrilled to have his dad home for Thanksgiving. They had been invited to share it with Dillon and his family, but Birk was grateful his dad turned them down. They appreciated the Andersons making Birk feel so welcome in their home, but alone time with each other was what both of them needed.

The kitchen was filled with a delicious aroma of sage and sugar. Mick poured his pumpkin mixture into the pie shell he had just finished fluting. Birk worked at the sink peeling potatoes. Ransom napped under the table, lifting his head to sniff whenever the oven door was opened and the smell of the roasting chicken wafted out.

"What time did you advertise the sale to start?"

Mick asked. "I see there's a chance of snow tomorrow."

"Ten," Birk said. "Everyone who's helping to set-up is going to get here by nine." Birk glanced over his shoulder to check his dad's reaction. "You think that's a good time?"

Mick nodded. "Yeah. That's a good time. Gives folks a chance to sleep in a little after the big holiday."

Birk continued. "The posters say the sale will go 'until dark', which is probably about five, I'm guessing. We'll keep those same hours for every weekend until Christmas."

Mick wiped his hands on a kitchen towel. "I have to head back to Dubuque Saturday, but I'm glad I can be here for your opening day tomorrow."

Birk smiled. "I'm just glad you got some time off. Do you know how much time you get for Christmas? We get a two week break from school."

Mick shrugged his shoulders and shook his head. "It's hard to tell with that outfit I work for, Birk. Let's just make the most of this holiday for the time being. Are things going okay for you at Dillon's?"

"Yeah, it's cool. They're nice. I've been going to chess club with Dillon, so that's kinda fun."

"Really? I don't remember the last time I played chess, but I remember I liked it."

"If you haven't played for a while, then maybe I could beat you," Birk said, smiling.

Mick laughed. "You probably could. Maybe after dinner?"

Just then Ransom crawled out from under the table and stretched.

Birk squatted down to stroke his nose. "I suppose all these good smells woke you up from nap number three, huh? Sorry, but it's dog food again for you, boy." Birk stood back up and grabbed the pan of potatoes. "The potatoes are ready to go on the stove, Dad."

"Good," Mick said. "The chicken and dressing are about ready to come out of the oven. That'll give us room for the green bean casserole and the pie. Hand me that meat thermometer over there, please."

Birk handed him the meat thermometer and got the aluminum foil out ready to cover the chicken. "Dad, did you know the Wheel family that is helping us tomorrow is the same family that bought our land?"

"Robert mentioned that on the phone last month." Mick raised an eyebrow and looked at Birk. "Does that make you feel better about the land, or does it make things more awkward for you?" Mick asked.

Birk shrugged. "Both, I guess. I know he isn't going to cut down the trees, so that makes me feel better.

A lot better. And Hannah always invites me over there, so that's cool. But it's also weird, being invited over to what was once our land." Birk glanced at his dad and shrugged. "It's not as bad as it could have been."

Mick squeezed Birk's shoulder. "Sometimes, things happen for a reason, son. I hope it keeps getting less weird for you. I'm going to fetch some firewood off the porch. I think it'll be a nice night for a fire."

And it was.

Birk and his dad had a relaxed and satisfying meal, but best of all, some long over-due conversations. They talked about school and work, friends and co-workers, would-be ghosts, the Wheel cabin and more. After dinner, they covered up all the left-overs, stuck them in the fridge, then cleaned the kitchen. While Birk cut two pieces of pie—and piled them high with whipped cream—Mick found the old chess board. They sat by the fire, ate pumpkin pie and took turns putting each other's king in check.

Birk couldn't stop smiling, even when he was mostly losing at chess. It was one of the best Thanksgivings he could remember.

~34~

SIGNS

Birk and his dad got up with the sun Friday morning to start setting up for the sale. The temperature had dropped into the mid-thirties and wouldn't get much warmer. Birk threw on his Carhart jacket, gloves, and stocking cap, then stepped outside into a holiday greeting card. The trees and grass were covered in frost, with just enough green showing through to contrast against the old red barn and slate blue sky. He zipped up his jacket and pulled up his collar.

He grabbed the two signs propped up on the porch and put them, along with a large hammer, in the back of the truck. He was extra careful with the sign Hannah painted, so he wouldn't scuff the fresh paint.

Both signs were mounted on stakes, ready to pound into the ground.

"Ready to go?" Mick asked, walking to the truck.

"Ready," Birk answered. "Let's go to Johnson's first."

They drove to the Johnson property at the end of Mason Road. Birk removed Hannah's sign from the back of the truck, along with the hammer. He placed the sign in the roadside ditch, with the arrow pointing straight down the lane toward his house. He pounded the sign until it was secure. "Can you see it from the road ok, Dad?"

Mick gave him a thumbs up. Birk hopped back in the truck and they drove back to their property entrance. Birk pounded the second sign right by their mailbox.

"Ok, what's next?" Mick asked.

"Let's drive up to the barn and pick up the saw-horses and rope for the parking sign," Birk said. "We'll get the measuring stick and pruning saws, too."

Dillon arrived on his bike in time to help set up the parking sign. "Dad's searching the garage for his pruning saws. He'll drive them over when he finds them."

"Okay. Hey, Dillon," Birk said. "Could you give me a hand with the kitchen table? I want to move it onto the porch to use as the check-out stand."

"Sure," Dillon said.

"Whoa," Mick said. "Don't you think a folding table would be a better choice, Birk? That table's solid maple, you know?"

"I know, Dad, but it will be under the overhang so it will be protected. This is what I want to use," Birk insisted. "I'll take full responsibility for it."

Mick scratched his head, then shrugged his shoulders. "Well, I guess this is your show. Let me give you a hand. It's pretty heavy. Hold the door open, would you Dillon?"

They positioned the table where Birk wanted it, then he went inside to retrieve one of the matching maple chairs. "There, that looks good!" Birk said. "It classes up the place, doesn't it?"

"It's just a porch, Birk. Just a porch," Mick said.

Birk went inside to retrieve the cash box, which he set on the table; the poster with the list of instructions and price information, which he hung on the porch wall behind his chair; and another piece of paper, which he placed on top of the table anchored under the edge of the cash box.

"What's this?" Mick asked, seeing the piece of paper Birk had added. "Table made by Mick McKenzie?" Mick chuckled. "Are you trying to sell our kitchen table now?"

"I'm just letting people know what you can do. Who knows? Maybe somebody will want a table just like this one and before you know it, you'll have enough orders to start your own business."

"And when would I have time to make all this furniture you're dreaming up orders for?" Mick asked.

But before Birk could answer, the Wheel family pulled into the drive. Hannah, her brothers, and Annie bounced out of the truck and each grabbed something from the back end to bring up to the porch. Robert and JoAnn followed with arms full of supplies.

Mick and Robert shook hands and introduced themselves, then Robert introduced Mick to his family and Annie.

"Call me Mick, please. Nice to meet you all and thank you for everything you're doing. Hannah, that's a great sign you made. If that doesn't lure in a crowd, then it just wasn't meant to be. And once they get a whiff of those cookies, I think we could run out of trees. Or at least cookies."

Everyone laughed, except Jamie. "Maybe I should have one now before the crowd gets here," he said.

"I like the way you think, Jamie," Mick said, laughing.

"I could use some help setting up the refreshment table," JoAnn said.

"I'll help, Mom," Wes said.

"Annie and I can help, too," Hannah added.

Robert walked back toward the truck. "I've got some saws I need to grab."

"Stack them on this bench with the rest of them," Mick said.

Robert stepped onto the porch with a handful of pruning saws. He glanced at the table and stopped to do a double take. He handed the saws off to Dillon and Mick, all the while staring at the table. He pulled off a glove and slowly ran his hand across the surface. He looked up at Birk. "This is a beautiful table," he said.

Birk was beaming. "I know, right?" Birk pointed to the sign he'd placed on the table. "Dad made it." Birk stepped away from the chair. "He made this chair, too."

Robert stepped closer and rubbed his hand across the finish on the chair.

Mick chuckled. "Birk was determined to make sure someone noticed that table."

"It would be hard not to notice. Maple, right?" Robert asked him.

"Right," Mick said. "Are you a wood-worker?"

"I've dabbled in it," Robert said. "But I've never made anything this fine." He looked under the table to study the joinery of the legs. "This is beautiful.The kids said you've been working in Dubuque. Do you have a furniture shop there?"

Mick snorted. "No, not even close, I'm afraid. This has never been more than a hobby for me, really. I used to work at the cabinet shop in town, but when they closed I had to go to Dubuque to find work."

Robert nodded. "So, the table and chair. I assume there are more chairs. Any other pieces?"

"Our house is full of them!" Birk couldn't help himself. "You should show him, Dad!"

Robert had a hopeful look on his face. "If you have time, I'd love to see more."

Mick chuckled. "Come on then. I guess we have some time before the crowd arrives." Mick ruffled Birk's hair as he walked by, then held the door open for Robert.

"And this is just a hobby, you say?" Robert asked.

Birk looked up to see Hannah smiling at him. It was clear she had witnessed the exchange. He smiled back, thrilled that someone else recognized the quality of his dad's work. But there was no time to dwell on it, because a vehicle was approaching the drive.

"It's almost ten," Hannah said. "It must be our first customer!"

"Oh, it's just Dad," Dillon said. "He's dropping

off the saws. I'll get 'em."

Ah, rats! Birk knew it was too good to be true.

"It's early," Hannah said. "Don't worry. They'll come."

Dillon pulled the saws out of the back of the truck. Boone waved as he drove away.

Dillon stacked the saws with the others. "What should we do now?"

Birk shrugged. "Just wait, I guess."

And so they did.

Wes and Dillon passed a football. Birk watched.

Hannah and Annie tossed a frisbee. Birk watched.

Jamie chased Ransom and Ransom chased Jamie. Ransom took off running for the fence line. *Rabbit, probably.* Jamie chased after him. Ransom started to bark at the fence. *Yep, rabbit.*

Robert and Mick finally came outside.

Mick squeezed Birk's shoulder. "What time is it, Dad?" Birk asked.

"A little after eleven."

Birk shook his head. "No customers yet and it's been an hour."

Birk thought his dad looked odd. "Birk, it's going

to be ok. Just relax and enjoy the day. Even if you don't sell a single tree. We're together and your friends are here. It's a good day."

"Come and play frisbee with us, Birk!" Hannah called.

"Maybe later," Birk answered.

"I'm going to run over with Robert to take a look at their cabin," Mick said. "That okay with you?"

Birk nodded. "Yeah. That's fine, Dad. Nothing's happening here anyway."

"Hey guys," Robert said. "We're going to go check out the cabin and then run into town to pick up some burgers and fries for everyone. We should be back by noon, ok?

"Sounds good," JoAnn said. "Would you get me a coffee, too?"

"One coffee," Robert said. "Aren't you cold sitting there? Why don't you wait inside until they need you?"

"No, I'm fine," JoAnn said. "I've got my blanket and my book. I just need the coffee."

"Got it. We won't be long." Robert said.

Birk watched as Robert and his dad drove away. He fidgeted with the items on the table, restacked the saws, and straightened his poster of rules for the third time. He plopped down on the porch steps, picking up rocks from the grass and throwing them back at the drive.

Hannah took a break from chasing the frisbee and sat down beside him.

"I was afraid of this," he said. "But I really wanted it to work. I'm sorry you've wasted your school holiday and all the days before today that you spent on it."

"It hasn't been a waste," Hannah argued. "Besides, we're going to buy a tree from you. Why don't we go check them out now? Mom! We're going to go look at trees. You want to come with?"

"You go ahead." JoAnn said, waving her book in the air. "I'm having trouble putting this book down."

Birk, Hannah, and Annie walked to the field to look at the trees. Nearly noon, and not a single sale.

~35~

A PRANKSTER REVEALED

Birk walked through the rows of trees with Hannah and Annie. He pointed out his favorites and taught them a trick for identifying a pine versus a spruce or fir.

"Wait!" Hannah said. "Let me see if I can do it. This one has clusters of needles attached to the stem so it's pine, right?"

"Yep," Birk said. "So what's this one?"

"Okay," Hannah said. "The needles on this one are single, not clusters, so it's either spruce or fir." Hannah tapped her lip. "Let me think."

"Feel the end of the needle," Birk said. "Is it sharp?"

"Oh, that's right. Yes, these are sharp. And I'm supposed to see if I can easily roll the needle between my fingers. These are easy to roll, so it's spruce?"

"Good job," Birk said. "So you must know what this one is."

"Let me try!" Annie said. "This needle is single, too, and it's soft, not sharp. It's flat so it doesn't roll. Does that mean it's a fir?"

"Right!" Birk said. "You guys are almost experts

now."

"My hands smell like Christmas now!" Annie said. "Oh, I love it. This is the kind I want. What is it?"

"Balsam fir," Birk said.

"Balsam fir. I need to tell Mom to get this one," Annie said.

"You might want to try this one first," Birk said. "It's a Fraser. Wait a sec." He looked towards the drive "I hear a car."

"It's our dads," Hannah said.

But it wasn't *just* their dads. It was a string of five vehicles. Birk, Hannah and Annie took off running for the drive. Wes and Dillon stopped passing the football to see what was happening.

Robert pulled the truck up by the porch. Mick hopped out with the food. Robert drove up by the barn and out of the way to make parking space for the two trucks and two cars that were behind them.

Birk and Mick greeted the customers. They briefly explained the process and price, gave them each a saw, and sent them on their way toward the trees. While Robert passed out the burgers and fries, Mick explained what they had encountered on the way to town.

"The sign at the end of Mason Road was pointed in the wrong direction," he said.

"What?" Birk said. "How could that be?"

"You set the sign just fine, Birk," Mick said. "It had been pulled out of the ground and moved. Whoever moved it obviously didn't have a hammer with them, because it was practically falling over."

"Why would anyone do that?" Birk asked.

"Who would do that?" Hannah asked.

"Well, that's just mean-spirited," JoAnn added.

"Probably that kid Ransom and I saw by the fence," Jamie said.

Everyone stopped eating and turned to look at him.

"What kid was that, Jamie?" Robert asked.

"He was over there," Jamie said pointing toward the fence line where Ransom had run earlier. "Ransom saw him first and barked at him. His bike was sorta stuck in the ditch, but he took off as fast as he could once he got the bike free."

"But you didn't recognize him?" Hannah asked.

"He looked familiar. I think he goes to our school, but I don't know him. If I saw him again, I would recognize him...and then we could arrest him."

Mick chuckled. "I don't think we need to go that far, Jamie. It wasn't really a crime to turn the sign around. More of a prank."

Hannah, Birk, and Annie all looked at each other.

"Hmmm," Annie said. "Now who is a prankster that goes to our school and is all *anti- Christmas trees*?"

"Nick Nadler!" Hannah and Birk said in unison.

"Anti-Christmas trees?" Wes said.

"Well, real trees, anyway. He was giving Birk a hard time when he read his paper about his family tree farm," Hannah explained. "Jamie, did the kid seem like he was more your age or my age?"

"Your age. He's about the same size as Birk. He rides a blue bike, wears a brown jacket, unzipped and had on a red sweater underneath," Jamie said.

"Wow. That's very observant," Mick said.

"He wants to be a detective," Robert said.

"Oh, and a purple baseball cap…backwards," Jamie added.

Hannah, Birk, and Annie looked at each other. "Nick!" they said in unison.

"He has a purple baseball hat and he always wears it backwards," Hannah said.

"What's his problem, anyway?" Annie said.

"Let's not spend too much time worrying about this Nick guy," Mick said. "We'll keep our eye on the sign so it doesn't happen again. Right now I hear another car coming. You guys better eat your lunch while you can."

Nick may have delayed the start of the sale, but it was in full swing now!

Once the make-shift parking lot was full, Mick directed vehicles to line up on the path to the barn. As one family finished their purchase and left, another would arrive to fill their spot.

Birk sold five trees before he was able to sit back and take in the scene around him. Families leisurely walked through rows of beautifully shaped trees. They rubbed the needles and sniffed the trees, then moved on to the next. Children laughed as they ran from tree to tree—sometimes stopping to hug one of the baby trees.

Wes and Dillon helped haul trees to the porch. Birk measured and priced them. Mick and Robert helped load and tie them, when needed.

One family of four approached the porch with two trees, a large one for the family, and a much smaller tree that the two little girls had picked out. While the adults tended to the business end of the purchase, the two little girls accepted cups of hot chocolate from Jamie.

The older girl blew on her hot chocolate and looked up at Jamie. "You have a nice farm," she said, shyly.

"Thanks, but it's not mine. It's his," Jamie said,

pointing to Birk.

Her little sister, lips covered in marshmallow, rocked back and forth on the heels of her bright red cowgirl boots. She looked over her shoulder at the field behind them, then squinted at Jamie. "Do you have a horse or a pig?" she asked.

"No," Jamie said.

"Then you don't really have a farm, do you?" she said, pursing her white lips.

"Missy!" her sister giggled. "He already said it's not his farm."

"Nope. It's not, 'cause that's why. But thank you for the hot chocolate," Missy said, now smiling.

Jamie looked at his Mom and rolled his eyes. "I think I need a break."

JoAnn laughed. "Oh please, don't leave. This is fun."

"For you maybe! I wasn't expecting these trick questions."

But the momentum soon picked up speed and the chance for a break for anyone would be hours away.

Hannah and Annie worked wherever they were needed, often times in the kitchen brewing up a new batch of hot chocolate, or fetching water for the thirsty laborers. They also walked the rows of trees to see if anyone had any questions. If they didn't know the answer, they ran to ask Birk. He had a quick response each time.

It was close to four o'clock when the snow started to fall, but nobody seemed to mind. In fact, it seemed to magnify the fun everyone was having. Children ran around with tongues sticking out to catch the snowflakes. Moms and dads snapped pictures with their cell phones, trying to capture the beauty of the moment. Trees flew off the lot. More customers continued to arrive.

"Looks like we might be working past dark," Mick said. He went in the house and came out with several strings of Christmas lights. Robert helped him hang them all around the porch.

Jamie clapped when they finally plugged them in.

"It's magical," Hannah said.

And finally, when the last truck pulled out of the drive—with two Christmas trees thrown in the back—everyone plopped on the porch in relief.

"Well, Birk. I don't think that Nick kid hurt you too much today," Mick said.

Birk smiled. "I think this was our best first day of sales ever. I'll know for sure after I count the money."

"I wish we had a pot of chili to offer you all," Mick said. "We have some left-over chicken and pumpkin pie we could warm up."

"Oh, goodness no!" JoAnn said. "We have plenty of Thanksgiving left-overs at home. But I think we'll get our tree tomorrow when we have better light to look around, if that's okay."

"That's a good idea," Mick said. "I have to head up to Dubuque tomorrow, but Birk will be here and Boone and his wife are going to help him. I don't want you paying for your tree, either. That goes for you, too, Annie and Dillon. We might not be able to pay you for all your help, but we can certainly offer you a tree."

Robert shook Mick's hand. "Thanks, Mick, but we were happy to help. It didn't feel like work at all."

"It was SO fun!" Annie said. "I want to come back tomorrow and help again!"

"Me, too!" Hannah said.

"I'll come back!" Wes said.

"Me, too!" Jamie said.

"Well, there you go," Robert said. "We had a great time and we're ready to help whenever you need us. And, Mick, I really enjoyed our chat. Get back to me as soon as you can."

Mick shook Robert's hand. "The pleasure was all mine. I hope to get back to you tomorrow, Robert."

BEST NEWS EVER

The saws and measuring pole were secured in the barn. The kitchen table and chair had been moved back inside the house. Birk decided to leave the Christmas lights plugged in a little while longer. He liked the look. He set the cash drawer on the table and sat down to start counting the day's earnings.

"I'll warm up the left-overs while you work on that," Mick offered.

Birk stopped. "Hey, Dad. What did Mr. Wheel mean when he said to get back to him soon. Was it something about the furniture you showed him?"

Mick grinned at Birk, "You might say that."

Birk looked eagerly at his dad. "Does he want to buy one of your pieces? Or order one made? He could tell how good you are. By the way, several people said nice things about the table!"

"Maybe I need to spend more time listening to you," Mick said. "What if I told you he wanted me to go into business with him? He's always wanted to have a side business for custom-made furniture and cabinets."

Birk couldn't believe what he was hearing. "Yes!

That would be so perfect! You'd be back home!"

Mick laughed. "I would."

"But, why didn't you say 'yes'? Why did you say you'd get back to him tomorrow?"

"Oh, I told him yes. You can be sure of that!" Mick said. "But I need to let them know in Dubuque. I can't just walk out on them. I would like to give them a week to find a replacement for me, but they may need me to stay for two. That's what I'll find out tomorrow when I go back up there."

Birk was ready to explode. "Dad, you might be home for good in two weeks? Maybe even one week?" He jumped up and gave his dad a hug. He thought of all he'd been through the past few months and how he once thought the worst thing was losing part of the family farm. But knowing he would soon have his dad back with him—in their own home—made him realize what was most important to him. "That's the best news ever, Dad!"

Mick chuckled as he hugged Birk back. "Looks like I'll be making furniture after all, doesn't it?" Mick ruffled Birk's hair. "And to think I tried to talk you into using a folding table on the porch."

Birk smiled up at his dad, happy to think he may have played a part in helping him get his new job.

"Thanks for sticking with your plan, son. And

now get back to counting your money while I warm up dinner."

Birk smiled all the while he counted the money… and re-counted the money. He realized he was so excited about his dad having a job in town that he was making mistakes counting. He kept coming up with an amount that was way too high. "Okay, I need to focus! One last time." But when he came up with the same amount as before, he finally believed it and wrote it in the tree journal. He went back through the pages of the previous years.

"This is our best first day of sales ever, Dad. Almost double what we made our second best year. I wonder why Grandpa never had the tree sale here."

"He probably thought it wasn't good customer service, but I think he would approve of what you and your friends accomplished here today, Birk. I suppose if the snow keeps falling, it could slow things down. City folks may be less inclined to drive out to the country for their tree if there's snow to mess with. Time will tell. But for now, you had a great day. I think you should go through those seedling catalogs and get an order in for spring planting."

"Yes!" Birk said. "Thanks, Dad!"

"Don't thank me. Thank yourself and your friends."

* * *

Birk got up early Saturday morning to see his dad off. He freshened Ransom's water, had a quick bowl of cereal, then got bundled up to feed the birds. When that was done, he and Ransom did a quick walk through the rows of trees left to harvest. Ransom mostly played in the snow and ate the snow.

Birk gave some of the trees a shake to get the snow off. He liked them covered in snow, but thought customers might prefer to see them in their green glory. He was happy to see the stumps were trimmed to the ground and wouldn't be causing a tripping hazard.

Just then he heard a vehicle pull in the lane. He thought it was early for Dillon and his parents, so was even more surprised to see Robert's truck pull up to the porch. Birk and Ransom headed toward the drive.

Robert jumped out of the truck and waved to Birk. "Just dropping off some helpers for you before I head to work for a couple hours. JoAnn sent me with more hot chocolate and cookies, too."

Birk walked to the back of the truck to help unload when he did a double-take. He watched as Annie, Hannah, Wes, Jamie, and a most unexpected guest exited the truck. This time he was wearing a stocking cap instead of the usual purple baseball cap.

"Nick?"

He shuffled toward Birk; hands shoved deep in his pockets.

Birk looked at Hannah and Robert for an explanation, but Nick finally spoke up.

"Hey, Birk. I came to apologize for yesterday. I was trying to be funny, but now I know it wasn't. I didn't mean to hurt your business. Sorry."

Birk glanced behind Nick. "Did they make you do this?"

Nick turned around and looked at the gathering behind him and shook his head.

"*He* called *me*, Birk," Hannah said. "It wasn't the other way around."

Birk shrugged. "Okay then. I accept your apology."

"JoAnn is bringing lunch out later, kids," Robert said. "We'll pick out our tree when I come to pick you up, okay?" Robert said.

"Okay, Dad," Hannah said. "Thanks!"

Robert started to get back in his truck, but Nick didn't make a move to go with him. "Aren't you catching a ride back with Mr. Wheel?" Birk asked.

Nick pulled gloves from his pocket and put them on. "I'd like to stay and help. You know. To make up for yesterday," he said.

Birk stared at Nick to see if he was for real. There was no sneer or goofy grin. Nick just stared back. "Is that okay?" he asked.

Birk shrugged. "Okay. You can help me move the table to the porch. Then we need to get the saws out of the barn and we should grab a snow shovel and broom so you can clear the steps and a path from the parking area. Do I need to send you down the road to check the sign, or is it where it should be?"

"The sign is where it should be, Birk," Hannah answered, smiling. "We stopped so Nick could brush the snow off of it."

Nick smiled sheepishly at Birk and nodded.

Birk and Nick walked up the porch steps.

"Nick, I've been meaning to ask you. Any chance you were at the old library on Halloween?" Birk asked.

"Huh? Isn't that a museum now? Why would I go to a museum on Halloween?"

Birk opened the kitchen door for Nick. He glanced back at Hannah and the gang and shrugged. "Just checking," he said.

~37~

BEST GIFT EVER

The days leading up to Christmas seemed to race by. School was dismissed on Friday, the week before Christmas, and wouldn't be back in session until the New Year.

Hannah and her brothers continued to help Birk and his dad on weekends. Surprisingly, so did Nick. Mick convinced the families to each accept a free tree for their help, but Birk knew better than to offer a tree to Nick. Even so, Nick worked hard to make up for his prank with the sign, so Birk decided to pay him with cash.

Hannah was working at the farm that final day of sales and heard Birk offer Nick the money.

"No, I can't accept it," Nick said.

"Go ahead, Nick. You earned it. Even if I deduct for the two hours that the sign was turned around, you still earned it."

Nick hesitated. "You could just give me a tree like everyone else."

"What? I thought you didn't like real trees," Birk said.

"But I never actually said that, did I? I was just giving you a hard time. We're getting tired of that dusty old artificial tree and Mom wanted me to buy one of yours. She gave me some money, so here, keep this."

Birk shrugged his shoulders. "I don't want your money. But come on. Let's cut your tree."

As they walked away together, Hannah heard Birk say, "Now you know to water it every day and make sure your lights are in good working order, right? Keep it away from any heat source. I don't want it to catch on fire and then you tell Miss Barrett you were right and I was wrong."

Nick chuckled. "Yeah, I know."

* * *

Hannah was so happy for Birk that his dad was back home with him and that his dad was doing work he enjoyed. Hannah's dad was equally happy that he found someone with Mick's talent.

"We've already got orders for two dining sets and a desk," Robert shared at dinner one night. "Once he gets more crew hired, he's going to do the cabinetry at the homeless shelter, too."

"That's great news! Did Mick say if he and Birk can make it for our Christmas Eve get together? Curtis will be here and Denny and his wife said they can make it."

"Mick and Birk will be here," Robert said.

Jamie looked at Hannah and smiled his big toothy grin.

Hannah felt her face turning red. She gave the slightest shake of her head towards Jamie and silently mouthed the words, "Stop It."

"Uh, Jamie," JoAnn said. "Do you want to help me set out the collection of snowmen after dinner?"

"Sure, Momma Jo!" Jamie said. "Did you get batteries for them?"

"I did. And I got enough for all those candles we found, too."

"Yippee!" Jamie said.

Once the dinner dishes were scraped and loaded into the dishwasher, JoAnn and Jamie unpacked the snowmen –large and small—and all the candles. JoAnn brought out several packages of batteries.

Robert exited down the hall to work in his office. Wes and Hannah were playing a game of chess in the living room.

"Okay, this is how you open the back on these," JoAnn said. She opened up the smallest of the snowmen. "This one needs triple-A batteries, like these here." JoAnn installed the batteries, closed the back and flipped the switch.The snowman's body suddenly glowed from within.

"Wow! Okay, let me do the next one," Jamie said. He followed JoAnn's instructions, closed the compartment and flipped the switch. "Ooh. Sweet! Set him right here by his little buddy. "I want to do this big one next!"

"Okay. That's probably C batteries. Let's open it up and see what it says," JoAnn said.

"That's definitely a bigger compartment," Jamie said. "Yeah and it says 'C' right there. We need two of them." He placed the batteries in the proper position, closed the compartment and flipped the switch. "Wow! His eyes light up!" Jamie turned the snowman toward JoAnn. "Look, Momma Jo!"

"Oh, yeah. I remember that one," JoAnn said. "Look at that. His eyes, his nose, his buttons, and even his hat light up. How about that?"

Jamie looked lost for a minute, staring at the back of the snowman.

JoAnn waved her hand in front of his face. "Jamie, are you in there?"

Jamie looked at JoAnn. "Can I call Curtis?"

"What? Now?" JoAnn chuckled. "I thought you wanted to help me. Are you bored already?"

"No. I'm not bored. I'll be quick about it and then I'll finish these," Jamie said.

JoAnn looked at her watch. "It's a little late, Jamie. He might be asleep already."

Jamie jumped up and ran to the window. He looked below at the alley three stories down, traced the fence of Curtis' backyard until he spied the kitchen window, a warm glow of light spilling out on the back porch. He looked back at JoAnn. "His kitchen light is still on."

JoAnn waved her hand dismissively. "Okay. Fine. Call him, but keep it short."

Jamie dialed the number, then stretched the phone cord as far as it would go into the hall. JoAnn heard Jamie whispering on the phone, but true to his word, it was a quick call.

"He's going to call me back as soon as he can," Jamie said.

"Do you care to tell me what this is all about?" JoAnn asked.

"Mmmm. Not just yet. Let's get back to work," Jamie said.

JoAnn chuckled. "Yes, sir!"

Just as they were closing up the final battery compartment on the final candle, the doorbell rang.

Jamie gasped, ran around the kitchen table,

through the living room, jumped over the ottoman and yanked open the door before Wes or Hannah had a chance to respond.

"What was that all about?" Hannah asked.

"Who knows," Wes said. "Sounds like Curtis is at the door."

Jamie glanced over his shoulder then whispered, "Curtis, I thought you were going to call." He stepped outside the door and shut it behind him.

When he returned, his face was red—just as red as his sister's face at its reddest.

"Jamie, what was that all about?" Hannah asked. "You look strange."

Jamie put up his hand to stop her from talking, walked past her and Wes, through the kitchen, and into the hall. He peaked around the corner and tried to get JoAnn's attention. "Pssst. Momma Jo. Come here," he whispered.

* * *

Christmas eve was a chilly thirty-two degrees. Light snow had been falling for hours, almost guaranteeing a white Christmas for Flinthills. The kitchen island at Horseshoe Hideout was loaded with veggies and dip, cheese and crackers, pickles and olives, Christmas cookies of every color and flavor, and a bowl of festive punch suitable for all ages. A big pot of chili was bubbling on the stove.

The majestic Fraser fir in the living room was aglow with lights and ornaments. Almost as beautiful as the tree, was the reflection it made against the darkened windows. Across the room, a roaring fire crackled in the fireplace. The smell of burning apple wood complimented the savory smells from the kitchen. Five stockings in assorted colors and sizes hung from the mantle. Jamie made sure all the battery-operated snowmen and candles were turned on.

At five o'clock sharp, the doorbell rang with the arrival of their first guest. Hannah, Wes, and Jamie all charged for the door. Curtis was the first to arrive. "Merry Christmas!" they greeted. Hannah took his coat, Wes took his hat and Jamie took his hand, leading him into the kitchen for a glass of punch.

"Merry Christmas, Curtis!" JoAnn greeted. "I hope your walk over wasn't very treacherous."

"No, not at all. The temperature is dropping, so the snow is staying pretty dry. Your home looks and smells delightful!" Curtis said.

Soon the other guests arrived and before long they were all seated at the table enjoying a warm bowl of chili and cheerful conversation. The grown-ups talked about the weather forecast and how soon they could try ice-fishing on Turtle Lake. The children talked about the prospect of sledding in the next couple of days.

"How did your Christmas tree sales compare to other years, Birk?" Hannah asked.

"This was our best year ever! Oh, and guess what? Dad told me to place an order for seedlings to plant in the spring and he's going to build a small shelter at the side of our drive that we can use as a check-out stand and hot chocolate station.

"We're going to keep the cut-your-own-tree model from now on. He also said if you guys want to help next year, you're going to get paid by the hour. Annie and Dillon, too."

"Wow. We get to have all that fun and get paid, too?" Jamie asked.

Hannah, Birk, and Wes all laughed.

"But not Nick, right?" Jamie asked.

"Oh! I forgot Nick," Birk said. "But if he wants to help again, he'll get paid, too. I don't think he'll be pulling any more pranks on me. I think he was just feeling left out and wanted to do something to get our attention."

After dinner and dessert, the kids watched a Christmas movie while the grownups cleared the table for a game of cards and a gift exchange. JoAnn told the kids it was something they did every year during their card game, so Hannah was surprised to see Robert hand an oversized envelope to Birk's dad as they said their good-byes.

"Was that Mr. McKenzie's Christmas gift from you, Dad?" Hannah asked.

"No. His gift was a new fishing rod and a tin of cookies from your Mom," Robert said.

Hannah thought it would be nosy if she asked for more information, but Jamie didn't mind asking.

"Then what was in the envelope? Was it a Christmas bonus?" Jamie asked.

Robert laughed. "No. Not a Christmas bonus. He's only worked with me for two weeks. It was just a little business transaction between the two of us. I don't think you need to concern yourself with that tonight. For now, I think your Mom has a surprise for you."

"What is it, Momma Jo?" Jamie asked.

"Well, when I was kid, we were allowed to open one gift each on Christmas Eve," JoAnn said.

"Yes!" Jamie said, clapping. "Can we, too?"

"Yes, you may," JoAnn said.

"Cool!" Wes said.

"But there's a catch," JoAnn said. "I pick out which gift you open. So, take a seat everyone. Let's see. Which one for Jamie? I think this one!" JoAnn handed him a large, awkward box.

"That's the one I would have picked, too!" Jamie said. "It's nice and heavy, like…" Jamie tried to shake the box. "Power tools?"

"What?" JoAnn said. "Did you ask for any power tools, Jamie?"

"No," Jamie said. "But it's okay if that's what you got me." By now he was ripping open the package. "Ice skates! Yeah, that's what I asked for! These are way cool! I'll look like a real hockey player! Check out the stripes, Wes!"

"Yeah, they're great, Jamie!" Wes said. "You can use those on Turtle Lake when it freezes."

"But you only skate where and when we say you can," Robert said. "Got it?"

"I know, I know. 'Cause the ice may be too thin and I could fall through," Jamie said. "I love these!"

"Okay. Now, for Wes. Robert, look in the coat closet, behind the coats." JoAnn said.

Robert pulled out a very long package, that could only be one thing. "A toboggan!" Wes shouted.

"Is that like a sled?" Jamie asked.

"Better than a sled!" Wes said. "This is like what the natives of northern Canada used for transportation. It's great! Thanks Mom and Dad!"

"You're welcome, honey. Now, this one is for Hannah!" JoAnn said, handing her a small box.

Hannah noticed the childish scrawl on the name tag. "But this says it's from Jamie." She looked up to see them all smiling at her.

"It is, but that's the one I want you to open tonight," JoAnn said.

"Me too," Jamie said.

"Me three," Wes said.

"It's unanimous," Robert said.

"This sounds like a conspiracy!" Hannah said, tearing off the paper. She lifted the lid, then gasped in disbelief. Her eyes glistened with unshed tears as she tenderly picked up the delicate garnet bracelet she thought she would never see again.

She looked at Jamie. "You found this? How? Where was it?"

Jamie took a deep breath and released his rapid-fire story. "So! I was helping Momma Jo put batteries into the snowmen last week, remember? And it was time to do the big snowman. It had a large battery compartment, just like that cat of Olga's with the eyes that lit up, remember? So, I put in the batteries, closed it, flipped the switch and it lit up just like that cat. Except the cat was creepy and the snowman is cute. But anyway, I thought what if that cat quit lighting up because the batteries were taken out so something could be hidden inside?

"So I called Curtis and he said, yes, he had the cat collection in his shop so he went over to the Wheel and Deal and opened the back of the big creepy cat and there was your bracelet!" Jamie finally took another breath.

"He's been dying to tell you that story for a week. Can you tell?" JoAnn said.

"Jamie, you are absolutely the best detective I know!" Hannah said. "And you kept that a secret from me for a whole week? You are getting so grown up!"

"Oh, and don't worry," Jamie added. "Momma Jo had the bracelet cleaned so there wouldn't be any Olga cooties left on it."

"And the jeweler said he can add length to the bracelet if you need it, Hannah," JoAnn said.

Hannah laughed through her tears. "Come here, you," she said, reaching for Jamie.

This time, Jamie leaned in. "Okay. Just so you'll quit crying." Hannah hugged him and planted a kiss on his forehead. "Okay! That's enough!" Jamie said, wiggling free.

"Thank you! Thank you, everyone. This is the best Christmas gift ever!" Hannah said.

~38~

REDEMPTION

Mick and Birk were greeted by a tail-wagging Ransom when they returned from the party.

"Hey, boy! Did you miss us? Huh?" Birk scratched Ransom behind the ears. "We missed you, too. Were you a good boy and left the tree alone?" Birk glanced into the living room to make sure their Christmas tree was still standing. "Looks like he behaved."

Mick chuckled. "He's learning, isn't he? That was a nice time tonight, wasn't it?"

"Yeah, that was fun. Did you know that building used to be an old warehouse? It's the same warehouse where Hannah and her brothers hid from their mean aunt when they ran away."

"Really? I didn't know that," Mick said.

"Yeah. They hid out on that same floor. They called it Horseshoe Hideout and that's what they still call it today."

"Well, how 'bout that? It's a beautiful space," Mick said. "I guess it's almost like they were meant to be there, huh?"

"I know," Birk answered.

"Speaking of beautiful places where you're meant to be, here's an early Christmas gift for you." Mick took an envelope from inside his coat and set it on the table.

Birk looked at it and then looked at his dad. "Isn't that the envelope Mr. Wheel gave you?"

"Yes, but it's for you. Sorry it isn't wrapped up all Christmas-like. I think we have some more Christmas paper, though, so I could wrap it first and put it under the tree…"

Birk laughed. "No! This is fine!" He opened the envelope and started to read. He looked up at his dad, puzzled. "Is this about the land?"

"Yes. I know it's a lot of legal mumbo jumbo, but this is what it means: The Wheels are keeping the lake-front clearing with the dock and their cabin. They are selling the woods back to us. But they will be yours. See?" Mick pointed to the document. "It says Birken McKenzie. If you ever decide you want to sell, give the Wheels a chance to buy it back before you offer it to anyone else. They want to make sure nobody goes in and starts cutting down the trees." Mick smiled. "And they know that you won't."

Birk gulped. "But how can you afford...?"

"The price was reasonable and I'm making payments. Some cash, but most of the payments will be in the form of furniture for their cabin." Mick smiled. "Those payments will be a pleasure to make."

Ransom whimpered and rubbed Birk's leg.

Birk couldn't believe what his dad had done for him. And he couldn't speak for the lump in his throat. He tried to smile, but he didn't think he pulled it off. He leaned into his dad's shoulder and buried his face. Mick wrapped his arms around him, patting his shoulder.

"I think that means you like it?" Mick asked.

Birk nodded, still not able to speak.

"Probably your best Christmas gift ever?" Mick asked.

Birk nodded.

"For me, too, son. Me, too."

acknowledgements

I have several people to thank for helping me get THE CHILDREN OF HORSESHOE HIDEOUT books into the world, starting with my parents, Robert and Joan Matthews, and my siblings, Roberta and Marla.

Though my mom passed away before book one was published, she gets credit for buying me my first set of paints and my first typewriter. She was every bit as kind and supportive as JoAnn Wheel, and would have been thrilled to know I finally finished my book.

Like Robert Wheel, my dad had his own construction company. To this day, my sisters and I love the smell of freshly sawn lumber and can't look at an abandoned building without visualizing a renovation (like the old warehouse in book one). Thanks for that, Dad, and for passing down your artistic ability and your love of fishing.

Thank you to my long-time critique partner, Ann Carter, for the gentle nudges to tell a better story. Thank you to beta-reader, Caleb, for the invaluable feedback. Thank you to multi-taskers Roberta and Marla for the critiques, copy edits, and overall words of encouragement. They were both cheerleaders in school and now they're mine.

Thank you to my sons, Matthew and Bryan, for the encouragement, constant humor, and invaluable artistic advise.

Thank you to my childhood friends and teachers who made growing up in my very own 'Flinthills' so special.

Cover art watercolor and graphite
Interior illustrations graphite

Published by The Painted Chickadee Publishing Co.
of Burlington, Iowa
thepaintedchickadee.com

First published in 2021

ISBN Paperback 9780578990170
ISBN Ebook 9780578990187

Printed in the United States of America

CPSIA information can be obtained
at www.ICGtesting.com
Printed in the USA
FSHW022008051021
85183FS